Lilian Faschinger was born in Austria in 1950 and holds a PhD in English Literature from the University of Graz where she worked for seventeen years. She has received literary prizes both for her own writing and for her achievements as a translator of such authors as Janet Frame, Gertrude Stein and Paul Bowles. Her debut UK novel, *Magdalena the sinner*, achieved widespread critical acclaim, with Shaun Whiteside's intelligent translation winning the 1997 Schlegel-Tieck Prize.

Lilian Faschinger lives in Vienna.

Also by Lilian Faschinger

Magdalena the sinner

Woman with Three Aeroplanes

Translated from the German
by Shaun Whiteside

Lilian Faschinger

First published in 1993 by
Verlag Kiepenheuer & Witsch, Köln

First published in the UK in 1998 by
HEADLINE BOOK PUBLISHING

First published in paperback in the UK in 1998 by
HEADLINE BOOK PUBLISHING

A REVIEW paperback

10 9 8 7 6 5 4 3 2 1

ISBN 0 7472 5849 X

Printed and bound in Great Britain by
Clays Ltd, St Ives PLC

HEADLINE BOOK PUBLISHING
A division of Hodder Headline PLC
338 Euston Road
London NW1 3BH

For Thomas Priebsch

LIST OF CONTENTS

the
globe

The rotating light on the ceiling casts patches of light on the talking, drinking, dancing people below. Luka dries the glasses and puts them upside down on the chrome surface designed for the purpose. He likes working behind the bar. His zone is marked out, he hardly needs to move, people come to him. He sees everything and is protected by the bar.

A beer, says the middle-aged blonde woman with silver glitter on her eyelids and sits down on one of the red stools. Luka looks at her briefly.

She is lonely. She's going to talk.

He puts a glass under the tap and lets the beer pour slowly out. When he puts it in front of the woman the foam runs over the condensation-covered glass. It's OK, says the woman, although he hasn't apologised. My cat likes beer. She gets drunk on it. My kitchen window is on the ground floor and looks out over a courtyard. All the cats in the neighbourhood visit me and my cat. They jump through the window.

Right, says Luka, and pours cognacs for two customers who have been sitting at the bar for a long time, kissing each other with their eyes half closed.

Hi, says the regular, swinging himself on to a stool. How are things? This is John, a friend of mine. He's a dancer. John, this is Luka, the youngest barman in the world.

Hi, says Luka and studies the dancer. He is a black

man, very light skinned, mid-thirties. His hair is cut short, his body medium-height and slim. The muscles in his neck are slightly protruding. He seems to be slightly drunk, his eyes are gleaming.

Hi, Luka, he says, and raises his hand as if making an oath.

Luka goes about his work and occasionally exchanges a few words with the two customers. The dancer ponders him unashamedly.

When does the bar close, he asks.

At two, says Luka.

The blonde woman is now speaking to the couple, who have stopped talking to each other.

And then the captain built himself a coffin, carried it on to the veranda and lay down in it, she says.

The couple stare at her, holding hands.

And the same night my cat was driven over by the car, the blonde woman goes on. The cards never lie.

We could go to my place later, the dancer suggests. All three of us. When you've finished your work, he adds and smiles.

Luka looks him in the eye. He could be my father. He's interesting. I never get to experience anything. I'm sixteen. I'd like something to happen.

The blonde woman's head bangs on the smooth plastic surface of the bar.

The dancer's flat is on the upper storey of a house in the city centre. It's very spacious, and sparsely furnished. Enormous black and white photographs showing the dancer in various body positions hang on the walls. On a gaming table covered with green felt there are many large glass globes. Luka takes one of them in his hand. Inside it is an open red parachute. He drops the globe from one hand into the other. It is cold and heavy.

I collect them, says the dancer. What I like best is transparent globes without coloured insides. They aren't easy to get hold of.

The regular is very drunk. He disappears into one of the rooms.

With the globe in his hand Luka walks through the open door on to a terrace with flowers and trees growing on it. It isn't cold. He sits down in a rattan armchair.

What do you want to drink, asks the dancer. Beer, wine, vodka, whisky, cognac.

Vodka, says Luka and weighs the globe in his hand. With orange juice.

The dancer goes back inside the flat. Luka hears a quiet rattle. He gets to his feet and leans against the low terrace wall. He sees the lights of the streets.

The dancer gently touches the back of his neck.

Here's your glass, he says and stands beside him against the wall.

What do you dance, asks Luka.

I dance on my own, says the dancer. I work out my programmes myself. I travel a lot. I'm from Haiti, I spend most of my time living here.

I live with my sister, says Luka. She's a teacher.

He drinks quickly. He has the glass in one and the globe in the other hand. The dancer brings him a second, then a third vodka. He touches his earlobe. Luka clutches the globe. The dancer glides his index finger over his neck and his chest. Luka stands motionlessly. The dancer gently reaches for his hand, wrests the globe from it and puts it on the wall. Luka totters. He sees the hammock stretched diagonally across a corner of the terrace. The dancer follows his gaze.

Do you want to lie down in the hammock, he asks. It's very comfortable.

He puts his arm around Luka's shoulders and guides him over.

It's from Haiti, he says. You have to get in crooked, and then it's fine.

Luka puts his glass on the floor and lies down. The hammock moulds itself to his body. He looks into the sky.

Where's Orion. My sister showed me where Orion is. A warrior with broad shoulders and a belt. I can't find Orion.

The dancer stands beside him and gently pushes the hammock so that it rocks back and forth. Then he too slips into it. His head is beside Luka's feet. His hands grasp his ankles, push up the fabric of his jeans and stroke his calves.

Luka stares fixedly into the black sky and doesn't move when the dancer's hands feel their way further along.

Luka walks along an avenue of plane trees. The morning is sunny, a cold wind is blowing. To the left above him rattle the blue wagons of the underground. In an open telephone box a man is shouting something in a foreign language into the receiver. By the telephone box a white woman walks up and down with a black baby on her arm.

6

His sister is standing in the kitchen in her dressing-gown.

Where were you, she asks. You're pale.

We had a party, says Luka.

The bar isn't the right thing for you, says his sister. She turns around, runs her hands over his shoulders and along his arms and kisses him on the mouth.

I was worried, she says. You must be careful.

Luka sits down at the kitchen table. His sister puts a bowl on the table in front of him. She pours him coffee out of a glass jug. He looks at her. A beautiful woman. In the morning she's warm and soft. Her eyes haven't quite opened, her hair falls into her face and over her shoulders. Her dressing-gown, carelessly closed, reveals parts of her body. She yawns and stretches by the window with her back to him. The contours of her figure are outlined black against the bright background. She lifts her arms and stretches her fingers.

He stands up, embraces her from behind and presses his mouth into her hair.

I'm going to bed, he says.

When he is walking down the corridor, the door of his sister's bedroom opens. A man wearing one of her shirts murmurs a greeting and goes into the bathroom.

The dancer steps up to the bar and leans on an elbow.

How are you, he asks.

I'm tired, says Luka.

Do you have time today.

No. I've got to sleep.

Tomorrow.

I don't know.

Let's go and eat. I'll collect you. Where do you live.

Maybe.

Where do you live.

Luka stands in front of the mirror in the bathroom and combs his hair. He uses small amounts of gel from a tin that he touches with his finger tips before running them gently through the hair on his forehead and temples. The bathroom is big and has one window with a lamp's wire frame hanging in front of it. His sister has taken it out of a skip and uses it to hang her many earrings. Luka wipes his fingers on a towel and holds big dangling earrings of black glass beads to his ears. He hangs them back on the wire frame and selects a tiny red spiral which he fastens to his right ear. Then he studies the series of flacons and vials belonging to his sister, takes a bright blue, beautifully carved flacon and sprays a little perfume on the inside of his wrist. He likes to be among all his sister's things in the bathroom. Hardly anything in the room belongs to him.

The doorbell rings. On the way to the door he sees his sister standing at the window of the corridor and looking down to the front door.

Who's that, she asks.

A man, says Luka.

The waiter brings stuffed figs.

Are you interested in photographs, asks the dancer.

8

I don't know, says Luka.

There's an exhibition near by that I'd like to have a look at.

The dancer doesn't take his eyes off Luka. After he has paid the bill they walk through a little park to a glass pavilion. The dancer leans against a tree and draws Luka to him by the lapels of his coat.

You, he says, and pushes him gently away again.

The photographs are by a Japanese photographer, and almost all of them show his dead wife. The portraits are like old paintings, the young, delicate woman has a timeless appearance. Apart from the portraits a series of photographs entitled The Journey is being exhibited. Luka walks closer.

They are enlarged contact prints with black perforated strips at the top and bottom as if taken at random. Pictures of clouds clearly taken from an aeroplane, the woman in the departure lounge of an airport, street scenes. The woman behind a street-sweeper in green with a green broom next to the green van of the street-cleaning department, the woman in a pink T-shirt at a flower-market, inside a room, probably a hotel room. Then again and again the screen of a television, coarse-grained pictures, the newsreader, faces of actors, advertisements, the test-card. Then the woman in the pink T-shirt in a corner of a room, against a window. Then the opened window. The view from the window on to the street far below. The woman in the pink T-shirt on the pavement, a small figure, lying on her belly. Then the television screen again.

The dancer walks over to Luka.

He's photographed his wife's suicide, he says.

He drove her to it, says Luka and looks at him.

The dancer takes his hand. Luka pulls it away.

Luka walks past the lift and runs up the nine floors to the dancer's apartment. Breathless, he leans against the white-painted door, runs his hands over it and kisses it. Then he rings the doorbell.

The dancer is wearing a long tunic with thin stripes and embraces him. Luka breaks away.

I'd like to have a bath. You can watch me if you like, he says.

The dancer goes into the bathroom and Luka takes the globe with the red parachute inside it and plays with it. Then he follows the dancer. The bathroom is very big and decorated with white tiles. A door and a big window with tall green plants in front of it lead to the terrace. Both are open. The oval bath-tub is in the centre of the room. Along one wall stands a white sofa. The dancer turns the water on. He tests the temperature with his hand and switches off the tap. Then he sits on the sofa and watches Luka getting undressed. He sits upright, his hands on his thighs. Luka slowly gets undressed and lays each item of clothing over the back of a chair. He is slim and almost hairless. A white scar runs parallel to his left shin. The dancer puts his hands between his knees. Luka climbs into the tub and sighs quietly as he immerses his body in the water.

Have you any champagne, he asks.

The dancer leaves the room and comes back with an opened bottle of champagne and two glasses. He fills the glasses and puts them on the edge of the tub. Then he moves an upholstered stool to the head end of the tub, sits down, hands Luka one glass and drinks from the other. He sits right behind Luka's head and studies the shaved back of his neck, his bony, freckled shoulders, the slightly protruding shoulder-blades, the bumps of his spine. Luka sighs again and stretches out in the tub. In the water his long body looks greenish.

Give me the sponge, he says.

The dancer picks up the big pale yellow sponge lying in the wash-basin and touches Luka's shoulders with it.

Leave me alone, says Luka sharply.

Leave me alone, says the dancer in the same tone, drops the sponge into the tub, looks at Luka's freckles, grabs his shoulders from behind and pushes his head briefly under water.

Are you mad, says Luka, when he has emerged again.

Are you mad, says the dancer in the same tone and walks out of the bathroom.

When Luka comes home at night a strange man is sitting drinking beer in the kitchen. Luka opens the fridge, takes out a bottle of vodka and goes into his room. Towards midday his sister knocks at the door.

Phone for you, she says. That man again.

I'm not here, says Luka.

He says it's urgent.

I'm not here, he says.

Luka walks up and down naked on the dancer's roof terrace watering the plants with a hose. A swarm of swifts drops squawking through sultry grey air towards the terrace and loops away in a high arch. Luka hears the dancer making a phone call in a foreign language and holds his breath. The tone is soft, tender. The phone conversation lasts a long time. Luka leans against the open terrace door and listens attentively. The dancer replaces the receiver and stays sitting on the sofa, elbows on his knees, hands folded.

Who were you speaking to, asks Luka.

My boyfriend, says the dancer.

Where is he.

In New York.

How old is he.

A year older than me.

An old man, says Luka and laughs. He takes the glass globe from the table, throws it in the air and catches it again.

Give me the globe, he says. I want to have the globe.

Take it.

Luka goes back out on to the terrace and lies down in the hammock. He weighs down his belly with the globe, depressing the flesh. The dancer walks after him, strokes his hips gently and reaches for the globe.

No, says Luka and protects the globe with both hands.

The dancer pushes the hammock violently.

Stop it, says Luka.

What do you expect, says the dancer.

Give me the tunic, says Luka.

The dancer pulls the tunic over his head and throws it on Luka's body. Luka laughs, carefully covers himself with it and takes the dancer's left hand.

And the watch, he says, running his thumb down its black face and undoing the strap. I want the watch.

The middle-aged woman won't stop talking.

Of course my cat can predict storms, she says. Let alone earthquakes. But the captain didn't like her. She tore one of his shirts to pieces, and he grabbed her by the tail and slung her across the flat. I threw him out, but he came back and brought beer for the cat.

Luka nods and fills two glasses to the mark with white wine. He glances up and sees the dancer coming down the steps and walking up to the bar.

It's not easy, he says.

The dancer leans against the bar.

Shall we see each other, he asks.

No, says Luka.

I'm taking a flight the day after tomorrow. I'll be away for two months.

Yes, says Luka and puts the glasses down in front of two men in dark grey suits.

There is a pause.

Is that all, asks the dancer.

Luka doesn't answer.

The dancer turns around and walks through the many guests to the door. Luka watches after him, then he leaves the bar and goes into the toilet. He leans his forehead against the wall covered with phrases and drawings and weeps. He washes his face above the wash-basin, takes the big black glass bead earrings out of his pocket and puts them on in front of the mirror. Then he goes back behind the bar.

No, it's not easy, says the blonde woman. Just to think that I was in the hospital with that miscarriage and the captain didn't visit me once. He didn't even look after the cat properly. I was losing pints of blood and he went to Zagreb with another woman. I should have known. It was all in the cards. Those earrings suit you though.

In the morning his sister comes into Luka's room and sits down on the edge of the bed. Luka's head is buried deep in the pillow, his legs stick out from under the blanket up to the knees.

I'm worried about you, she says. You don't say anything. You're so thin.

She starts stroking his ankles and calves.

Luka sits up abruptly.

Leave me alone, he shouts.

His sister sees the earrings in his ears, gets to her feet and walks to the window. There she turns around.

I knew it, she says. It's that man. You have no idea. He's experienced.

Shut up, says Luka. Just shut up.

What do you look like, she says. Look what you look like.

Luka turns slowly sideways, takes the glass globe from the little cupboard beside his bed and throws it through the room with all his strength. The globe narrowly misses his sister's head and smashes the windowpane. Shards of glass fall clattering to the parquet floor. The eyes in his sister's head are closed.

beautiful things

A sound wakes Lechner. He lifts his head.

The deer, he thinks. They're in the garden again.

Without switching on the light he gets up, walks to the window and pushes the closed curtain aside. It's dawn outside. A light grey strip lies on the horizon to the east. On the patch of lawn in front of the house stand two deer. They lift their heads.

What are you doing, says Lechner's wife and sits up in bed. Why are you waking me. You know how badly I sleep. I only just got to sleep. I had to take a sleeping pill. I can't get to sleep without pills.

Be quiet, says Lechner. The deer are there again.

The deer, says the woman. They're destroying everything. This house. This miserable house. We should never have built this house.

Be quiet, says Lechner, leaves the room and picks up the air rifle which leans against the back wall of the built-in cupboard in the hall beside a few winter coats. It's always loaded. The barrel is cool. Lechner goes back into the bedroom, carefully leans the rifle against the wall and quietly opens one wing of the window. The deer are standing beside the rose-bed.

They're eating the rosebuds, thinks Lechner. The beautiful buds of the roses.

What are they eating, says Lechner's wife. What are they eating this time. They eat everything.

Be quiet, says Lechner and raises the rifle. He takes aim at the left rear flank of the big animal. His hand is steady. He pulls the trigger. Silently, the deer he has hit leaps the hedge surrounding the property. And the second animal jumps over the hedge and has disappeared. Lechner turns around. He's about to put the rifle back in the cupboard. Then he thinks again, leans it against the wall of the bedroom and gets back into bed.

There's no point, he thinks, and turns towards the side of the marriage bed facing away from his wife. They keep coming back. You'd have to kill them. Why do they come all the way into the garden. They get enough to eat in the forest. They're getting cheekier all the time.

His wife's voice gives Lechner a start.

Get up, says his wife. I got up an hour ago. Get up, will you.

Lechner doesn't answer. He looks through the window and sees the sun behind the high, leaning beech tree. He's glad he decided to put two big windows in the bedroom.

The garden gate won't shut, says the woman and leaves the bedroom.

Lechner's eye falls on a photograph on the bedside table. It's an old photograph. It shows his wife and himself with their three daughters. The three daughters are grown up now. They don't come often and don't stay long. What a surprise, thinks Lechner. He wouldn't be able to stand it long in this house if he hadn't built it. He picks up the photograph and looks at his youngest daughter's face. He's sometimes talked to his youngest daughter. He looks at his wife. She was beautiful, he thinks. They were never happy, he thinks. There was a time when everything was better, he thinks. He doesn't understand his wife. He doesn't understand why she won't give up. Leave him alone. Why she won't stop talking.

Lechner thinks that he would have liked a son. He would have shown that son lots of things. He would have talked to him. He wouldn't have sat dumbly among the women, the talk about wool and buttons and shameless men who leave their wives, about children and fruit and pearl necklaces. He's sorry that these things don't interest him. Nothing about women's things interests him. He would have liked to leave his wife. He admires the men with the courage to leave wife and child. Who refuse to go on listening to all the talk.

Lechner picks up the little portable radio that always stands on the bedside table and turns the dial without switching it on. Nothing interests him, he thinks. He sees the rifle against the wall. He likes shooting deer, he thinks.

Lechner goes into the garden to mow the lawn. On the way he looks into the open kitchen and sees his wife sitting on a chair with her knitting in her hands. He quickly goes down the stairs. He gets the lawnmower out of the workshop and turns on the engine. He slowly walks with the lawnmower over the green patch in front of the house. He walks up and down. The lawnmower is noisy. Why is he walking up and down with the lawnmower, thinks Lechner. Why isn't he somewhere else.

He sees his wife coming out of the house with a bowl in her hand. He sees her hard, sad face.

The garden gate won't shut, says his wife as she walks past.

Lechner says nothing and turns around at the wall of the house.

I have to do everything myself, says his wife and bends down to the plants. We should never have built the house.

Lechner bumps the lawnmower against the trunk of one of the little fruit trees planted in a straight line. He curses quietly.

His wife stretches up and picks big beans from the tall wooden poles. She fills a bowl with the beans. Then she walks back to the house along the path laid with bits of stone paving.

The deer have eaten the young lettuce, she says. They eat everything.

Lechner eats the meal that his wife has put in front of him. While he eats he reads the newspaper beside the plate on the table. He sees the date at the top of the page. Today is his wedding anniversary, he thinks. He got married thirty-nine years ago, he thinks. He didn't like getting married. But saw no other possibility.

In the newspaper Lechner reads that a young man in America has fired into the street from a tower and killed lots of people. Lechner would like to be in America. The land is spacious in America, he thinks. You have a lot of room, he thinks. You get some peace.

He sees his wife coming out of the bedroom with a

white plastic basket full of wet washing. She is walking slowly. Her walk depresses him.

Lechner gets the garden shears and walks to the front of the house. He starts cutting the hedge. His wife hangs up the washing.

My back hurts, says his wife. You know that very well. You know my back hurts. I mustn't stretch. I mustn't bend. You know that.

Lechner says nothing.

The garden gate won't shut, says his wife.

Lechner throws the garden shears into the grass and walks into the house, up the stairs, past the door that leads to the bedroom. His eye falls on the dents in the door. Whenever he sees them he thinks of the evening he locked himself in the bedroom and his wife wanted into the bedroom. She beat the door with a heavy thick glass ashtray until he opened up. Lechner wonders why they don't buy a new door. A new door is expensive.

Lechner sits at his girlfriend's place drinking tea. He doesn't like being at his girlfriend's place. His girlfriend is strange to him. But he doesn't know where to go when the rage rises in him. His girlfriend sits opposite him at a little table. She's the same age as his wife. He has no relationship with her. He would like to have one, but he hasn't the confidence. He's afraid his girlfriend might become like his wife.

Lechner looks around the room. The room is small and full of souvenirs from his girlfriend's travels.

His girlfriend has a quiet voice. When he's telling a story she listens. She is a widow. It's hard for Lechner to hold the transparent tea-cup in his fingers. His girlfriend talks and smiles. Lechner doesn't listen attentively. He isn't interested in what she says. He's so tired.

I've got to go, says Lechner and stands up. He bumps his head on his girlfriend's ceiling-lamp. He often bumps into things in her flat. The things in her flat are very small.

Lechner prolongs the journey home. He doesn't want to go home. He doesn't know where to go. He walks past his brother's house and rings the doorbell. His brother and his wife aren't at home. In the early darkness Lechner walks on. He walks along a path lined with apple-trees. He thinks that he got married on the same day as his childhood friend, who has been living in a big city in the neighbouring country for thirty years. His friend has written to him, but Lechner never replied. He didn't know what to write. Sometimes he writes postcards to his youngest daughter. He signs them with the words Your Father. He likes doing that.

Lechner walks into the bar of a pub on the way to his house. A few men who know him greet him with loud voices. They offer him a beer. Lechner quickly finishes the beer and orders another one. He's afraid that his wife is standing in the door in her light blue housecoat. He's afraid that his wife is lying on the sofa in her light blue housecoat. He's afraid of her.

His fear vanishes after the second beer. Lechner orders a third. He talks a lot and quickly. The men listen to him and laugh. Lechner tells funny stories. He tells the story about the deer. He elaborates on the story about the deer.

There was this great stag in my garden in the full moon, he says and makes a gesture.

Lechner orders a round of schnapps for the men. The

men are his friends, he thinks. Not friends like the friend who went away, but friends. He hands the schnapps glasses to his friends. Let's drink to my wedding anniversary, he says and raises his glass. It's my wedding anniversary today.

A little later Lechner leaves the pub and walks the short journey to his house in the darkness. He sees the blue light of the television glowing in the distance.

He takes off his jacket and sits down in front of the television some distance from his wife. On the screen a black policeman with a pistol in his hand is walking behind a red car that he's using as a shield.

How's your whore, his wife says suddenly. Is your whore well.

The black policeman aims his pistol at a young man who is holding a beautiful woman around the neck with one arm. The young man has pushed the woman in front of him. He is holding a revolver to the woman's temple.

Lechner's wife starts shouting.

Why don't you stay at your whore's place, she shouts. Stay at her place if it's so nice there.

A second, white policeman comes from behind at the man who's holding the woman by the neck.

Calm down, says Lechner quietly. I was in the pub. Calm down.

The second policeman disarms the man.

His wife won't stop shouting.

You've been drinking, she shouts. You've been drinking again. You drink everything away. We could have built two houses with the money you've drunk away.

Lechner stares at the screen. He doesn't see what is

happening on the screen. He doesn't hear what his wife is shouting. He thinks that he would like to see his friend. He thinks that his friend understood him. He thinks that he will write to his friend.

Lechner walks out of the room. He leaves the door open a crack.

Lechner is woken by a blow to the back of the head. Instinctively he draws in his head and protects it with his hands. It takes him a little time to realise that his wife is hitting him.

Are you mad, he shouts and tries to hold on to her hands.

His wife doesn't stop. She tries with all her power to break away. She manages to bury her fingernails in the skin of his temple. When he touches his temple with his hand he feels moisture. He looks at his fingers and sees they are covered with blood.

You're crazy, he says. You're completely crazy.

How can you sleep, the woman yells, when I can't sleep. How can you sleep peacefully when I'm tossing and turning. You don't know how terrible it is.

Lechner's heart beats. He's afraid of the rage within him. He sees the rifle leaning against the bedroom wall. The rifle can't kill a person.

The woman has twisted out of his grasp and starts hitting him again. Lechner grabs her by the throat and throttles her. He has big, strong hands. His wife resists. Lechner looks at his hands. His hands look as though they don't belong to him. He thinks that he must stop if he doesn't want to kill his wife. He notices that she's no longer resisting him. He wants to stop pressing, but his hands are still around her throat. With a great effort he manages to take his hands from her neck. His wife sinks back on to the bed.

Lechner stands up and picks up the portable radio and the photograph. He picks up the previous day's clothes from a chair, lays them over his arm and leaves the bedroom. He goes into the bathroom, puts his clothes on, washes his face, sticks a little plaster over the wound in his temple, cleans his teeth and combs his hair. He gives himself time. He looks into the mirror and sees the white-haired head of a man in his late sixties. He puts a few things in his plastic sponge-bag and closes the zip. He walks out of the bathroom. When he passes the bedroom he hears his wife groaning. He walks into the living-room, takes a little key from one of the jugs standing in a row on the cupboard and opens the top drawer of a chest of drawers. From it he takes some bank-notes, a passport and a letter. He puts the money into the passport. He closes the drawer again and takes a big brown and white checked travelling-bag from the wardrobe. He puts the portable radio, the sponge-bag and an umbrella in the case. He puts on his shoes and an anorak. He puts the photograph, the passport and the letter in the inside pocket of the anorak and walks down the stairs into the garage. He opens the garage door, walks to the garden gate, opens the garden gate, goes back and sits down at the wheel of the car. He drives the car out of the garage and through the garden gate. He stops, walks back, shuts the garage door and then the garden gate. He gets into his car. He drives off. He screws up his eyes. He can't see so well these days.

He turns into the road leading into the city. He drives to the end of the village where he was born. He drives out of the village. There are no lights on the road here. There is little traffic, a lorry overtakes him from time to time.

Lechner thinks slowly. He thinks clearly. He thinks that he's been exploited. He thinks that he has worked and had nothing for it. He thinks that he has liked people and had nothing for it. He thinks that his wedding anniversary has been over since twelve midnight.

As he approaches the sharp bend he thinks that he could simply drive straight on. If he drove straight on he would crash down a steep slope to the saw-mill. He has seen several cars lying there before. Years ago he wondered whether he should drive straight on at that bend. In those days his youngest daughter was still a child.

Lechner drives around the sharp bend. He drives into the middle of the road to clear the bend. With some pleasure he thinks of the possibility of someone coming towards him. He takes the bend well. He sees the lights of the city in the plain. He moves on towards the city. He drives to the city station. He leaves the car locked in front of the station building and walks into the hall with his almost empty travelling-bag. On the large round white-faced station clock it is just before five o'clock. The noise of his stout brown shoes echoes loudly on the stone floor of the big space. He runs his left index finger from top to bottom of the sheet with the departure times fastened to the wall. He walks to the ticket counter and buys a ticket to the big city where his friend lives and where he himself stayed during the war. He asks for a second-class one-way ticket.

He sits down in the waiting-room. On one of the

wooden benches a man in a black suit is sleeping on his back with his feet crossed. A big black hat is lying on his belly. Next to the man a young couple sit leaning against one another. A woman walks into the waiting-room. It is hard to tell her age. Her legs are bare and dirty, she is wearing pink plastic sandals. Her face is scratched, her hair is dishevelled and twisted into two little horns over her forehead. The woman, who looks like a little devil, is talking to herself quickly and quietly. She utters sharp cries. She stands next to Lechner. She looks attentively at Lechner and goes on talking. Lechner understands a word from time to time but he can't put them together. He only understands that she's talking about him. He takes the portable radio from the travelling-bag, quietly switches it on and puts it to his ear. The woman, cursing and complaining, raises her voice and leaves the waiting-room. A violent eruption of Vesuvius within the next fifty years is within the realms of possibility, says the male voice on the radio. This view is shared by the overwhelming majority of scientists.

Lechner thinks that he has seen photographs of active volcanoes and barren, dark volcanic landscapes. He would like to walk on the black stones of a landscape like that. He would like to walk where nothing grows and where no human being can live. He thinks there are landscapes like that in America. Lechner nods off and keeps falling into holes in his half-sleep.

The loudspeaker announcing the arrival of his train wakes him from his dozing. He picks up the travelling-bag and makes for the platform. It is light now. A group of young people is waiting for the train. From their behaviour and their words Lechner concludes that they are heading for their final school examination. The young people are talking and laughing. When the train pulls in they say their goodbyes to their relations and friends.

Lechner gets into the train and pushes aside the door of a closed compartment. Sitting in the compartment is a young woman with a girl about three years old. The girl has no shoes on. Her red rubber boots are under the seat. She looks up at Lechner and smiles at him. Then she walks through the open door in her thick stockings and starts running up and down the corridor. The young woman quietly admonishes the child. The child goes on running up and down. Lechner lifts his travelling-bag on to the luggage rack, walks through the door and up to a closed window in the corridor. A wide road runs parallel to the tracks. Superimposed with the cars are the vague outlines of his wife in her light blue housecoat. He doesn't think his wife is dead.

Catch me, calls the child from the other end of the corridor. She runs so quickly at Lechner that he spreads his arms and bends his knees. The child runs into his arms. He picks her up and lifts her into the air. The child laughs and starts drawing circles on the dusty window with her index finger.

Look, says Lechner. All the cars.

I want to get down, says the child.

Lechner puts the child back on the floor. She runs along the whole length of the corridor to the glass door separating the two parts of the carriage. There she turns round. Again she runs towards Lechner. Again Lechner picks her up. They repeat this game a few times. Lechner notices that each time she runs, the child glances into one of the compartments and then runs on more quickly. The child takes him by the hand and pulls him to the compartment. Lechner sees young soldiers in grey uniforms sitting in it.

Who's that, asks the child.

Those are soldiers, says Lechner.

The child runs to the glass door and turns around. Lechner walks to the other end of the corridor and spreads his arms out to catch the child. He puts her on his arm.

They're dangerous, whispers the child.

The soldiers, says Lechner.

Yes, whispers the child. The soldiers. The men. They're all dangerous. You're dangerous too.

Stop running, says Lechner. You've got too hot.

The child's mother steps out of the compartment and fetches the child. She apologises for the child annoying Lechner. She puts the child's coat and little red boots on her. She gets off the train with the child.

They're all dangerous, they're all dangerous, the child calls out as she gets off. You're dangerous too.

Lechner sits down, leans his head in the corner, pulls his anorak up in front of his face and tries to sleep.

He doesn't know how much time has passed when a man in a uniform asks for his passport.

Lechner looks out of the window and sees the slightly coloured mixed forest, the pools, the boggy meadows. He recognises the landscape. He thinks that he drove through this landscape fifty years before in an over-filled train. He knows that it was shortly before Christmas. He had four days' leave from the front. A young soldier from the village on the other side of the lake went with him. The train stopped a few times, and they had to get out and seek shelter from low-flying raids. Lechner remembers throwing himself into the sharp-edged grass and startling a hare. He remembers the face of the soldier from the village on the other side of the lake. They completed the last twenty kilometres of the journey on foot, in the middle of the night. They walked together to where the lake started. There they separated, and the soldier walked on the southern side to his village, while he himself continued along the northern side. Now and again they called out each other's names across the lake.

The signs of the city appear at the train window. Lechner takes the light travelling-bag and makes for the door. When the train stops he presses down the handle and climbs on to the platform. The station is very large, and Lechner loses his bearings for a moment. A huge glass roof curves above him. He walks along the platform and enters the large hall.

The escalator takes him down to the exit. Beside him people are going up on another escalator. A young man in blue working overalls dashes past the other people. A little way behind him runs a second man, holding a knife.

I'll slit you open, he shouts. If I get you I'll slit you open.

Lechner, who has put his right hand on the rail of the escalator, notices that his hand moves rather faster on the rail than the rest of his body.

Next to the exit he sees the word BANK in big white capital letters. He goes to the counter and hands his savings book to the clerk. The clerk opens it, flicks through it and looks at Lechner.

I'm sorry, but you can't make withdrawals from your savings book in this country, he says.

Lechner says nothing. Then he takes the bank-notes out of his passport.

I'd like to change some money, he says.

Go to the cashier, says the clerk.

Lechner changes the money and steps into the open. There is dense traffic in the square and in the streets in front of the station. Lechner remembers a different city, a city of ruins, a silent city. He walks through this strange city as he once walked through the other city. He doesn't recognise anything.

He's hungry. He walks through an open door draped only with a white plastic curtain, above which the word ASIA is written in red letters. He sits down at a big empty table covered with a red table-cloth. Beside him, on a shelf, stands a small aquarium. The inside of the aquarium has a bluish-green glow. A waiter asks Lechner what he would like to order. Lechner orders a beer and a recipe with a name unfamiliar to him. He looks at the little fish in the aquarium. They are golden fish and black fish with long tails that drift through the water like the trains of a dress. The plants, bile-green in the water, float back and forth. Air bubbles rise and form a little whirlpool at the surface. Lechner sees two of the black fish suddenly attacking one another. Lechner thinks that he has been cheated. He knows it. He thinks that people like himself are cheated of their lives from day one. He sees the weaker fish hiding behind a small stone. He looks at his hands. They are broad and covered with blotches. It isn't easy to move his fingers. Lechner thinks that he has always set great store by cleaning and caring for his hands. That he enjoys filing his nails. That he has enjoyed brushing the shoes of all the members of his family, covering them with shoe-polish and polishing them. Lechner notices that one of the goldfish is dead.

The waiter brings the beer and the food, vegetables and rice. Lechner eats quickly and bows his head towards his plate. A coloured man with a bouquet of roses wrapped in Cellophane comes into the room. He holds out the bouquet to him and smiles at him. He asks him to buy a rose. Lechner buys two roses and puts them in his travelling-bag.

Lechner pushes the empty plate aside and takes the letter and photograph out of his jacket pocket. On the back of the letter is his friend's address. Lechner takes the letter out of the envelope and reads. The letter was written six years ago. It says in the letter that he is still working as a tool-maker and earning a lot of money. That his son's girlfriend is expecting a child in a few months. That he has just been on holiday in Sardinia with his wife.

Lechner remembers that his friend and he had been in love with the same girl, and that he had been luckier than his friend. That he didn't understand the girl's language and that they called her the Scottish girl. While he tries to call to mind the appearance of the Scottish girl his eye falls on a delicate landscape of trees and a little castle under a glass cover. He wonders what material the landscape is made out of. He thinks it is a light, soft wood. He pays the bill and picks up his bag. On his way out he stops by the landscape under the glass cover and looks at it. He sees a little heron. He recognises that the material is cork. He thinks that there are beautiful things.

He asks the first passer-by who comes towards him

directions for the street where his friend lives. The passer-by, an elderly man with a long-haired white dog, gives him the information. He points to a flight of steps leading to the underground.

You have to go five stops, he says. When you come out of the station walk straight on and then take the first street on the left. That's the street you're looking for.

Lechner walks down the steps to the underground. He tries in vain to get through the turnstile. A man behind a pane of glass calls to him that he has to buy a ticket. Lechner buys the ticket, stamps it, walks through the turnstile and gets into the blue train that has just pulled in. At the same time a middle-aged woman gets on. She is dressed in black, has gold teeth and a bright and flowery headscarf. She moves to the end of the compartment.

I'm desperate, she exclaims in a high, monotonous voice. My husband died three weeks ago. I have five children. They're all small. I have no money. Help me. Give me money. Help me.

She walks past the passengers and holds out her cupped hand. Her hand is dirty. Lechner puts a coin in it. He sees that he is the only one who has given the woman anything. At the next stop the woman leaves the train, and Lechner watches her get on to the next compartment, take up her position at the same place and start talking.

Lechner gets out and walks into the open. He finds the street and his friend's house number. His name is not on any of the name plates. Lechner presses a bell.

Hello, says a voice from the intercom.

Lechner asks whether his friend lives here.

I don't know the name, says the voice in the intercom.

Lechner repeats the question and gets no answer. He presses a second button. No one answers. He presses a third button.

Hello, who's there, says a girl's voice. Lechner voices his question again. He gets no answer when he repeats the question. A fat woman leaning out of a window on the first floor asks him who he's looking for. He says his friend's name.

He did live here, says the fat woman. With his wife and his son. But that was at least four years ago.

Thank you, says Lechner, turns around and walks back to the underground station. In the square in front of the station he sits down on a stone bench. People walk quickly past him. He looks at the people. He sees some who have been cheated as he has. He takes the letter out of his jacket pocket, stands up, bends down and lets it slowly slip through the rust of a grid set into the asphalt. Then he sits down again. He looks at the photograph. The photograph is a little bent. The colour of the photograph is yellowish, the edge serrated. His daughters and his wife smile at him. His own picture smiles at him. His youngest daughter wears a white blouse with a broad collar. Her hair falls to her shoulders. Lechner turns the photograph around. There are faded lines on the back, a division as on postcards. He puts the photograph back into his jacket and crosses the square. It is growing dark. Neon signs light up on the roofs of the tall buildings.

He walks into the big department store on the other side of the square. It has no windows. It is brightly lit. The individual floors are arranged around a big, high inner space with a brightly coloured glass roof. Lechner sees the balustrades of the four floors above him. He walks slowly between the stalls on the ground floor. Smartly dressed women in white coats with long red fingernails sell make-up and perfumes. Lechner looks at the various shapes of the glass bottles. He walks past a stall at which men's perfumes are sold. He thinks that his youngest daughter has always given him a perfume for Christmas. He thinks about the big argument he had every year at Christmas with his wife. The salesgirl turns her back to him. He picks up a deep blue bottle with the inscription MUSTANG and slips it into the pocket of his anorak.

He takes the lift to the first floor. The lift attendant wears a red uniform. He is unusually small. Lechner strolls through the women's fashion department, then through the rows of suits, jackets and coats for men. He touches the sleeve of a light camel-hair coat. Some distance away a sales assistant is serving a customer. Lechner runs his stiff fingers over the smooth, shiny material of the grey and burgundy housecoats. Ties hang on a stand. Pura seta/pure silk it says on little fabric labels. Lechner takes a black-and-blue patterned tie and drops it into the same jacket pocket.

He goes up the stairs to the second floor. On the shelves stand tins of fruit and fine vegetables, jars of pickled mushrooms and plums and bottles of wine and spirits. Sweets are arranged on large tables. Behind illuminated glass vitrines stand white-coated salesmen, cutting big hams into almost transparent slices, which they hold up to the customers. Lechner approaches one of the shelves, picks up a blue tin with a picture of pink crabs with long feelers and puts it into another pocket of his jacket.

He gets on to an escalator and takes it to the basement.

There he walks up and down between the shelves and stops at the tools department. He sees the blue metal toolboxes, the screwdrivers with red and yellow handles, the hammers with smooth, light wooden handles, the gleaming spanners arranged by size. He sees a spanner that he needs, looks around and puts it in his trouser pocket.

He takes the escalator to the ground floor and looks at the clock on the wall with the red illuminated numbers. He is surprised that the store is still open. He walks through the wide door into the open air and is prevented from walking further by two men who appear on his right and his left. They take him by his underarms and lead him back into the store. There they walk down the steps with him into the basement. A few customers look around at them. The two men lead him into a little room. One of the men goes and comes back immediately with a well-dressed, grey-haired man.

We have watched you stealing a number of times, says the store manager, and asks Lechner to open his bag and take off his jacket. When Lechner does not comply with his instruction, the two men take off his jacket. They find the perfume, the tie and the tin. Then one of the two men runs his hands over him and finds the spanner.

The store manager asks Lechner for his papers. Lechner hands him his passport. The store manager looks alternately at the passport and at Lechner's face.

What are you doing here, he asks.

I wanted to visit a friend, says Lechner. But my friend doesn't live here any more.

The store manager gives Lechner back his passport.

Since you're only here temporarily we won't press

any charges. Of course you must pay for the goods you have taken.

He goes with Lechner to the cash-desks in the various floors, where Lechner pays for what he has stolen. Then Lechner is allowed go.

Lechner doesn't leave the department store. He takes the lift to the fourth floor. There he looks down over the balustrade. He sees the smartly dressed women with their long red fingernails from above. The women are very small. He sees the enormous, glittering chandeliers hanging from the glass dome. He sees the lights of an aeroplane far above him, on the other side of the glass. He takes the photograph from the inside pocket of his jacket and looks at the four women and the man. He stretches the hand with the photograph over the balustrade. He drops the photograph and watches after it.

finger-hopping

Put your hand on the table.

The girl smiles and looks at the boy across the white table-cloth.

Put your hand on the table, he says again, looks at his watch and leans his head back so that his cheekbones stand out.

The girl's smile deepens and leaps to her eyes. Her eyes brighten.

Come on, give it to me, he says, and draws a paper-wrapped toothpick out of a little glass container in the middle of the table. He starts to tear open the wrapping.

She lowers her eyes and turns them towards her left hand, which lies on her thighs. Then she raises it, places it on the edge of the table and moves it slowly forwards without taking her eyes off it. Her smile remains on her face with its lowered eyelids.

Do it, he says, and darts the toothpick into the table-cloth.

She spreads the fingers of her hand. On the middle finger she wears a thin gold ring with two drop-shaped blue stones. The setting for the third stone is empty.

The boy pushes aside the beer-glass, looks at his watch and draws the hand closer to him. Looking into her face he sends the toothpick jumping, at first slowly, then more and more quickly, from one space between her fingers to the next, constantly returning to the one between thumb and forefinger. The girl keeps her hand still. She doesn't take her eyes off the speeding toothpick.

The pale man. The hand fast as lightning.

The boy performs the hand movement with concentration, and it's a long time before he sticks the toothpick into the skin between the middle and the ring finger. She laughs out loud, reaches for the beer-glass and drinks the last drops.

It's bleeding, she says, holding out her hand. Look.

Blood slowly drips between the two fingers, becoming a tiny hemisphere. She puts her hand to her mouth and licks it.

Let's go.

The boy looks at the time and gets to his feet. He is in his early twenties, not very tall, of rather delicate build, and with smooth black hair, shaved at the nape and falling over one eye. His face is broad, almost rectangular, with pronounced bones. The girl looks at him.

Fire salamander. Its tongue shoots out.

They walk under the black sky. A man stands bent over a newspaper lying on the pavement.

Algae blossoms in Istria, he reads out loud.

They laugh. The girl is about the same age as the boy, tall and red-haired.

Where are we going, she asks.

To your place, he says. I don't feel like sitting in the café any more. I'd like to see your flat. I'd like to eat something where you live.

She stops.

Come on, he says.

They wait for the night bus. Next to them a man falls from a bench and hits the asphalt.

Leave him, says the boy, when she's about to go over to the man. He's just drunk. Here comes the bus.

I don't want you to come with me, she says.

You're coming now, he says, gets in and pulls her into the bus. And you're not sending me away when we get to the front door.

They sit down behind two black men in American military uniforms.

Protecting the penguins, it makes me sick, says one, in English.

I know exactly what you mean, answers the other soldier.

She looks out the window. She turns her head.

I've told you about him, she says. Try and understand.

I don't understand anything, he sings quietly, and slowly shakes his head. I don't understand anything. I don't understand anything.

They get out and walk along the street that runs parallel to the suburban train-line. On the left the scaffolding of a gas-holder rises into the sky. The girl looks silently at the ground and quickly starts walking.

The fear. The lightning-quick fist.

I want a glass of wine, she says.

Let's drink it at your place.

I have none at home. There's a wine bar over there.

It's late.

She walks to the bar, pushes open the door and turns around on the threshold to look at him. He is standing some distance away with his hands in his trouser pockets, his face turned away. The furniture and the panelling are almost black. A pinball machine glows from one corner. She orders the wine and sits down.

Watch out, he said to her on the first evening, a few days before, and, with a grin, prodded his index finger in the air. Then he noticed her staring at him, understood when she said, with a smile and wide eyes: I'm dizzy. They were in the café, he was sitting with his back to the wall, his legs stretched out on the bench. And then, when she shuddered: Don't be scared. The café was empty apart from the woman behind the counter and a man in a white overall scattered with flecks of paint.

She orders a second glass, drinks quickly and doesn't notice the boy coming over to her. Only when he sits down beside her and looks at his watch does she become aware of him.

Come on, let's go, he says.

She pays, and they leave the bar together and walk to her house without speaking.

You're going to do something to me, she says, and stops walking.

I'll never do anything to you, he says, and puts his finger on her nose.

She opens the front door and they get into the lift, which sinks a few inches under their weight. At the door of her apartment the boy grins.

The worst is behind you, he says. The lift. As good films tell us.

The girl stares at him and sits down on the stairs beside her door, which lead to the next floor.

I don't want to, she says. I can't.

Stop it. Come on. I want to see the flat. I'm hungry. You're going to have to open the door sooner or later. You're just putting it off.

Without looking at him, she hands him the bunch of keys.

Go in. I'm staying here.

He unlocks the door, opens it wide and goes into the dark. She hears him walking about in the apartment, sees his silhouette against the window. She doesn't move. After a while she slowly stands up, follows him and closes the door to the flat. She turns on the light in the sitting-room.

Sit down, she says. I'll get you something to eat.

He stands in the middle of the room.

I'll give you one more minute, he says with a smile, and stretches.

She goes into the kitchen, puts ham and cheese on a plate, cuts a few slices of bread and places everything, along with a glass, a bottle of mineral water, butter and cutlery, in front of him.

You're afraid, he says, and brushes his hair out of his face. She sees his wide, high forehead, with its widow's peak in the middle.

No.

He points at her with the fork. Don't lie.

Not much.

Eat something.

I'm not hungry.

Eat. I can't eat if someone's watching. Eat now.

She takes a slice of ham between thumb and forefinger and puts it in her mouth. He eats slowly, and looks at his watch a number of times. The room is in darkness, the only light is in the hall and the kitchen.

Let's go into the other room, he says.

She follows him into the darkness and lies down beside him on the bed. They lie outstretched on their backs. Then he leans on his elbow and begins to stroke her face with the other hand. She puts her face into his palm.

Don't move, he says.

She closes her eyes. His hand moves slowly over her face. Then it slides down further. She sobs and reaches for his body.

No. Don't move.

He stands up, climbs on to the bed and puts himself above her. Then he raises one leg and puts his foot, at lightning speed, lightly on her belly, making her twitch. He leaves it there for a while, then jumps from the bed, switches on the light and starts walking around the bed.

Now you can see what kind of man I am, he cries, pulling the corners of his mouth downwards. What kind of man. What a man. Just brilliant.

What's up with you, she asks. Sit down. It's OK.

He walks up and down for a while, then sits down on the bed. She wraps her arms around his shoulders from behind, he lets her do this and lies back against her body.

Soft as butter, he whispers. This is the moment. Stick the knife in my back. It's time. Why don't you do it.

It's OK, she says, and holds him. Lie down. Sleep here.

It didn't happen, she thinks tiredly, and kisses him lightly on the back of his neck.

No, he exclaims. I have to go. I have to go straight away.

She remembers. The fire salamander crept across the village street. She bent over it and saw that it was injured. One side was torn open and bloody from the head to the abdomen. But who will kill it, she thought. Then she raised her right leg and trod on it with her trainer. She felt the big creature twisting beneath her foot, and trod on it again, several times, more firmly. Her foot felt the life leaving the salamander. While she was doing this she looked at a cartwheel hanging on the dark wooden wall of the house along the street. She didn't stop until it had stopped moving. Without looking, she ran up the grassy slope beside the street. There she looked at the sole of her trainer. Its treads were filled with a greyish red mass. She spent a long time wiping the sole against the stalks of grass.

Should I go, he asks.

She stands up, goes into the bathroom, slips into her red dressing-gown and smiles at herself in the mirror.

How beautiful I am. How young I am. Red cheeks. Gleaming eyes. He's weaker. I should have known.

Yes, go, she says. I want to sleep. I'll see you down to the front door.

the man
in the
chimney

The sun has risen behind the house. It shines through the small barred window into the big room where the two women are sleeping in a wide bed. There is nothing on the dark, uneven board floor. The room is rectangular in shape. The bed stands along one of the room's narrow sides. A few metres away from it is a small iron stove in the form of a tall cylinder. The stovepipe runs along the whole long side of the room. On the other narrow side a wooden bench stands along the wall, in front of it a square wooden table. There are two wooden doors set into the walls. They enclose wall cupboards in which old books are stored. Parallel to the bed, some metres away, stands a second, long and narrow wooden table. St John's wort is drying on it. Between the small windows hang a number of *verre églomisé* paintings, blurred portraits of women. The women's eyes are very large, their hands and lower arms painted black. It looks as though the women are wearing black gloves reaching to their elbows.

I can't paint hands, Eva has said and looked past Magda.

Magda doesn't believe it.

Magda turns around in bed and bathes her face in a rectangle of light. The warmth on her cheeks and her brow wakes her up. She doesn't open her eyes, but looks at the red behind her eyelids. The cat lies warm and heavy on her feet. Magda moves her feet and the cat stands up, opens its mouth wide, presses its paws against the bed-cover and walks across her body. It licks her lower jaw, curves its back and jumps from the bed. Magda opens her eyes.

He's coming today. Today's the party.

Magda slowly turns her face to the right. She sees part of the back of Eva's blonde head.

Magda sits up and sets her feet parallel to one another on the board floor. She sits there like that for a few minutes. Then, barefoot in her white linen shirt, she walks into the kitchen and, as she walks, she looks at the tall sheet of mirrored glass leaning against the wall in the landing. She makes coffee, takes a thick ceramic bowl from the wooden shelf on the wall, pours herself coffee and milk and walks on to the balcony with the full bowl.

Between the leaves of the tall plane tree in front of the house the sky is blue. In the night it has rained, water is dripping from the branches. The house is surrounded on three sides by steeply rising vineyards. The border with the neighbouring state is fifty yards away.

She finishes her coffee, takes two large watering-cans from the kitchen and walks down the stairs. The meadow in front of the house is wet with rain. At the well she puts the watering-cans down, opens the little wooden door, picks up the long-handled pail and dips it into the dark, walled water until the jugs are full. She closes the little door, lifts the cans and walks back to the house. On the way she puts them down and picks up little twigs and branches that the wind has torn from the tree in the night. She makes a little pile by the wall of the house, steps back and looks at the front of the house. It is a large house, three hundred years old, which once belonged to a seminary, now on the other side of the border. A heavy stone arch frames the green painted door, with blooming oleander bushes in pots on either side. The cat pushes through the crack of the door and wraps itself around the woman's legs. Their neighbour, working on the vines, calls to his son. Magda talks to the cat, picks up the cans, pushes the door wide open with her shoulder and walks through the porch. The cat follows her and runs up the stairs. On the half-landing Magda puts the cans down again. There are two heavy hooks in the whitewashed arch of the ceiling, which used to support a pole for drying clothes. She slowly walks to the upper floor with the cans and puts them beside the walled oven. Then she pours milk into a bowl and puts it down for the cat. She walks on to the landing, picks up the light metal washing table, carries it to the balcony and puts it in the sun. Then she fetches a jug and pours water into the washing bowl. She steps out of the linen shirt, washes without soap and cleans her teeth. She hears a sound and looks to her side. In a long light blue nightshirt Eva is leaning in the frame of the balcony door. She yawns and stretches her hands out in front of her.

He's coming today, she says. Your friend from the city.

The two women walk into the nearby wood to pick mush-rooms for lunch. On the way they pass a walled shrine dedicated to St Isidore. The portrait of St Isidore stands out against the light green background. There is a dried bunch of flowers in a beer-glass on a ledge below the saint.

In front of a farmhouse an old woman stands bent over in a garden. When Eva greets her she stands upright and walks to the fence separating the garden from the path.

Did you know, she says. Our neighbour's son cut off four fingers with the machine. On his right hand. They took him to the city. They sewed the fingers back on.

Magda looks at her hands.

But he'll never be able to work like before, says the farmer's wife and turns to the plants.

The two women walk on.

Do you know what they call us in the village, says Eva and laughs. The two madwomen. But they don't do anything to us.

They jump over a small stream at the edge of the wood. Black beetles crawl on large rag-like leaves in the shade beside the water. Sharp-edged blades of grass cut into the skin of their calves. Their feet in their trainers sink a little into the boggy earth.

We have no husbands. We have no children. We spend all summer living alone in the big house. What are they supposed to think, says Magda.

They walk across the forest floor covered with a layer of dry pine needles. Their footsteps ring hollowly as though a big cave was opening up beneath the ground. As if they were walking over a void.

The two witches, says Eva and laughs again. She pulls Magda along by the hand for a while.

Herb Paris, she says, pointing to a dark blue sphere surrounded by four leaves on a tall stem. It's poisonous.

The women search their way across the forest floor. They lose one another briefly, then find each other again. Next to a rotten tree-stump Magda sees the glow of something yellow. It's a big chanterelle. Beside it, half hidden under the needles, are lots of smaller ones. Magda cuts the big chanterelle off just above the earth with the knife she has brought with her and smells it. She doesn't give a start when Eva touches her on the shoulder. She hasn't heard her coming.

Eva holds up a purplish mushroom.

Russulas are edible as well, she says. She puts the russula in her wickerwork basket.

Let's go down the slope, she says. Ceps grow there.

The women move carefully over the slope. Magda slips on the smooth needles and falls over. Eva helps her stand up and brushes the dark hair out of her face. They walk on. When Magda is about to pull a cep from the soil she notices that she has lost her knife in the fall. She walks back and looks for the knife. She never goes into the forest without a knife. She looks for it for a long time. She doesn't find it. Little white moths tumble about in the semi-darkness as though they are lost. Sunlight falls through the foliage, great shafts of light with insects visible in them. The light makes the drops of water sparkle on the pillows of moss.

From time to time the women call each other by name. They are reassuring themselves.

A spider's web blocks Magda's path. She lifts her right hand, bends her fingers slightly and tears it from top to bottom with a sure movement of her hand. The big spider runs along the back of her hand. Magda shakes it off.

The two women prepare the meal. Magda sits down at the table and frees the mushrooms of earth and decaying matter with a little knife. Then she cuts it into small pieces. She is happy at the sight of the bright cuts.

Eva stands at the oven melting butter in a big black iron frying pan. She watches a finely sliced onion browning in the melted butter. Her eyes fill with tears. Magda walks over to her with the mushrooms. She slides them into the pan. Eva kisses Magda on the cheek. They stand at the oven and watch the volume of the mushrooms quickly reduce as the water evaporates. The cat comes into the kitchen.

Carrying the little knife Magda walks down the slope, out of the door and past the plane tree into the little garden. Crooked posts half sunk into the soil surround the garden, where herbs, lettuce, tomatoes and marigolds grow. Big bushes of forget-me-not flourish on the flower beds at the edges. Magda cuts herbs. The cat, which has followed her, plays with an empty snail-shell. Magda goes back, chops the herbs and adds them to the mushrooms.

Eva has spread a white cloth over the little table on the balcony and put out plates, cutlery and glasses. The two women sit at the table and eat. Magda sits on a small wooden bench. Above her on the wall hangs a stag's head. It isn't a real stag's head, it's an imitation stag's head with big antlers. The stag's head smiles. Between the antlers there is a birds' nest. The young birds have flown.

The women are tired from the meal. They go into the room and lie down on the wide bed. They lie in each other's arms. They go to sleep.

Later they set off. Some distance away the path leads through a forest. Eva points to tall plants with purple blossoms growing along the roadside.

That's wild orchid, she says.

Halfway along the path they meet a young man. The man is wearing a beige suit and says *Buon giorno*. The two women walk on with a sense of having put something dangerous behind them. Holding each other by the hand they cross the shade of the forest. They emerge from it on to a hill. They screw up their eyes into slits so as not to be blinded by the sun. At the highest point of the hill they see a wayside cross. Above the Christ hanging on the cross there arches a metal roof painted blue. Beneath his feet, nailed over one another, a statue of Mary inclines her head to the side. She is considerably smaller than the figure of Christ and looks up to a similar, correspondingly smaller roof above her head.

From the hill, not far away, a little lower in the valley, a village can be seen. The women take the path in that direction. They walk past a house with a big empty dovecote in front of it. A dog on a chain runs at them barking, until the chain is pulled tight.

That's the sculptor's house, says Eva. The dog is always on a chain. He isn't vicious.

She walks slowly up to the barking dog. She whispers calming words. The dog stops barking and stands at the end of the chain with its muscles tensed. Eva reaches out her hand. The dog doesn't move. She strokes the dog's head. The dog lets her do it.

The women walk on and reach the first houses in the village. They are old houses, painted shades of yellow. From a narrow street a procession comes towards them. Little girls in white dresses try not to get their black patent shoes in the previous day's puddles. Their faces are serious; artificial wreaths sit on their heads. They are carrying little woven baskets full of blossoms. With their transparent white gloves they reach into the baskets and scatter the red and white peonies in the street. Some of the blossoms float in the puddles. People watch the procession from the windows. They have put vases of peonies on the windowsills. The heads of the peonies are heavy and bend the stems a long way down. In the windows there are also brass lamps with burning candles on embroidered mats that hang over the masonry in a semi-circle. Two girls turn towards Eva and Magda and giggle.

When I was a child I went along as well, says Eva. All that mattered was the white dress. The evening before I put it on my bed with the gloves, my stockings and the garland and put my shoes underneath. I pretended to be pious, but it was only the white dress that mattered.

The peony blossoms, says Magda. As children we tore the petals off the geraniums in the flower pots and stuck them on backwards on our fingernails. We moved carefully so that they didn't fall off, pursed our lips and rolled our eyes like the ladies from the town.

The women nod to the two girls and walk on to a little station, half covered by an orange building net. The signal turns green. The area manager with the red cap staggers out of the door.

He's always drunk, says Eva. He's been moved here from the next town. He lives with a foreign woman who's much older than he is. He drinks schnapps.

The short train from the city pulls in. The women stretch and crane their necks.

There he is, says Magda.

A man has got out of the last of the blue and white

carriages. He is dressed in black and wearing a wine-red, wide-brimmed felt hat.

Magda pulls Eva with her by the hand and walks up to the man. The man embraces her. Eva doesn't let go of Magda's hand. The man kisses Magda on the mouth.

This is Eva, says Magda. Eva, this is Leonhard.

I'm hungry, says Leonhard.

First let's show you the mausoleum and the castle, says Magda. We'll eat later.

They walk along the stream to the church and knock on the door of the vicarage. The verger opens it and gives them the big key to the mausoleum. Magda takes the key in her hand.

They walk up the hill to the mausoleum. Eva walks behind Magda and Leonhard. She sees Leonhard putting his arm around Magda and kissing her. She hears Magda laughing. Visitors without a key are waiting outside the mausoleum. They walk into a cold, dark room. On the dusty floor there are stacks of tiles and a few sarcophagi. Eva trips over a cable and almost falls. The voices of the visitors echo in the room.

Let's go, says Magda, and asks the visitors to follow them outside. She locks the door.

On the summit of the hill is the castle. They walk into the courtyard. Leonhard leans over the well that stands in the middle of the courtyard. It is boarded over. Against one wall of the courtyard firewood is stacked up in a tall, wide pile. Eva stands on tiptoes at an iron door with a little opening. There are motifs of intertwining hands on the door.

Come here, she calls. You can see into a garden.

The other two walk over to her. All three look through the little opening into an overgrown garden. Magda stands in the middle and puts her arms around Eva's shoulders and Leonhard's waist.

Have you got anything for me to eat, asks Leonhard when they have arrived at the house.

In a minute, the women say. Let's show you the house first.

They walk through the house with him and show him the rooms. They climb a narrow flight of wooden steps to the attic and open the little door. Warmth and the smell of wood come out to meet them. Leonhard looks through the opening into a big dark room.

This is where the dormouse lives, says Eva. You hear him in the night. He runs up and down.

You must see the cellar, says Magda. They guide him around the house to an old door studded with big nails. The cat runs after them. The door isn't easy to open. They walk down the narrow cellar steps. The cat walks two steps with them, then pulls back its right front paw, which has just begun its next downward movement and hovers in the air over the third step, and stops. There is a smell of damp. Leonhard looks up to the ceiling. He is standing under a high arch on a cold, impacted-mud floor. He waits until his eyes have grown accustomed to the dark. The big cellar is empty apart from the shadow of a wooden rack with wine bottles lying on it. He thinks he can see a few wicker baskets stacked inside one another.

The women approach him in the darkness and giggle.

One of them touches him from in front, one from behind. Leonhard steps aside.

About a hundred years ago two women and a man lived in this house, says Eva. Both women loved the man. So they decided to kill him. They stabbed him and hung him up in the chimney. The smoked corpse was found forty years ago.

There's no need to be afraid, says Magda to Leonhard and laughs. The women push him to the cellar wall. Leonhard stands with his back to the wall and presses the palms of his hands to the rough surface. Again the women giggle and press themselves to him. Then they run up the steps.

It was just a joke, says Eva with a laugh. It was just a joke.

Leonhard stays leaning against the cold wall. He is very hungry. He doesn't move. Then he breaks away from the wall and walks slowly up the steps into the open.

The women put the mushroom dish in front of Leonhard. Leonhard has taken his seat beneath the stag's head. Eva sits on his left, Magda on his right. They watch him eating. Leonhard has barely room to lift his lower arm and bring the spoon to his mouth.

Do you like it, they ask him. You do like it, don't you.

The sun is hot. Eva and Magda have carried two sun-loungers down the slope and opened them up in the meadow behind the house. They have taken their clothes off and are sunbathing. Magda lies on her back. One of her knees is bent. Her eyes are closed and covered by the back of her right hand. Her dark hair hangs over the back of the sun-lounger and touches the tall grass. Her skin is tanned. Eva lies on her belly. Her face is turned to the side. Her hands dangle on both sides of the sun-lounger and play with the grass. Her skin is very pale.

Leonhard comes round the corner. He has had a look at the garden, the shed, the orchard, the vine. Before he can retreat, Magda opens her eyes.

You can lie on the blanket, she says. It's nice in the sun.

Leonhard hesitates. He sees Eva slowly turning on to her back. He sees her pale skin and her blonde hair. He takes off his clothes and lies down on the soft blanket that the women have spread out on the grass. He is very white, with little body hair. He spreads his arms and sighs. A gentle breeze blows across his skin and through the tall trees and bushes along the meadow. Leonhard looks into the sky. A big bird circles above him.

You must protect yourself against the sun, Eva says to Magda. She picks up a blue plastic bottle lying in the grass. I'll put the sun cream on you, she says, and rises from the sun-lounger. Leonhard turns his gaze towards her. She sits down next to Magda and applies the sun cream with slow, circular hand movements. The cat sits between the women and Leonhard.

Leonhard has sensitive skin, says Magda. Don't you, Leonhard. You have to put the cream on him. He needs to be protected as well.

Turn around, says Eva to Magda. Turn around.

Magda turns on to her belly. Eva distributes the cream on Magda's back. She takes her time.

Leonhard's skin will burn, says Magda.

Eva stands up, kneels in front of Leonhard, who is still lying on the blanket with his arms spread, turns the blue plastic bottle around and lets white cream drop on to his belly. Leonhard reaches into the fluid and draws circles around his navel with his hand.

Thanks, he says. Thanks. I'll do it myself.

Eva lies down on her back again. It's quiet. From the direction of the vineyards they can hear a man's voice calling. A wind-wheel for scaring birds starts clattering slowly, then more quickly. The cat makes a rapid movement. It has caught a cricket and chews it to pieces with a crunching sound.

The three get ready for the party. Eva stands in the spacious porch in front of the pane of mirrored glass against the wall. The glass is half clouded. She is wearing a long blue dress. The zip at her back is open and reveals her bare skin. Magda is standing behind her trying to close the zip. The blue fabric has jammed in the little hooks. Magda calls Leonhard for help.

Leonhard comes out of the guest-room in his shirt-sleeves. The two of them set to work on the zip. Their fingers touch each other and Eva's back. They manage to free the material. With a tug Leonhard pulls the zip closed. The blue dress is tight on Eva's body. Eva doesn't say thank you. She runs a comb through her hair, then paints her lips blood-red with a lipstick.

Leonhard follows Magda into the hall. Magda puts on a black pair of trousers and a black pullover. Leonhard stands at one of the windows watching her.

Do you fancy Eva, asks Magda. She's beautiful.

I fancy you, says Leonhard, walking over to her and embracing her. You're beautiful.

Magda dives under his arms and walks to the long wooden table.

Help me, she says. I'll show you something.

They lift the table-top with the drying St John's wort and put it on the wide bed. A game of skittles is hidden under the table-top. Magda picks up a nearly circular wooden ball and puts it in a groove in the table. Then she takes a long cue and puts it to the ball. She pushes the ball towards the nine wooden skittles, one of which is slightly smaller than the other eight. Four skittles fall over, including the little one. She hands Leonhard the cue and says:

You try.

Dressed in dark colours, the three walk along the country road that runs along the ridge of the hill. The sun is low, the valley is in shadow. To the left and the right are vineyards. Leonhard sees a farmer driving up and down on a little vehicle between the vines planted in straight rows. He sees the green container on the vehicle spraying a white liquid on the grapes. Eva notices his gaze.

It's poison, she says. They spray the vines several times. It doesn't work without poison.

From the hill they see the house and the big plane tree. The plane is the highest tree for far and wide. Eva stops.

When the former owner of the house died, the tree fell ill, she says. Shortly before her death the owner said: When I die the tree will die too. But the tree didn't die. For two years it had no leaves. Last year the leaves were small. This year the leaves were as dense as ever.

The three walkers pass a little whitewashed chapel. The door is open, they walk in. The right side wall of the chapel is covered with paintings. Magda looks at them attentively. It's a cycle made up of a large number of paintings. The murals have been well preserved. In one of the childish-looking paintings Eve is growing out of Adam's rib. In another Magda recognises St George and his armour and, at his feet, the dead dragon.

Eva stands in front of a statue of Mary in a little niche. She has lit a long white candle and folded her hands. She appears to be praying. She kneels on the wooden stool in front of the statue of Mary and puts her face in her hands.

Leonhard stands, arms dangling, in the middle of the chapel. He looks around. He doesn't know what to do. He's bored. He looks at the women lost in contemplation.

Halfway there the three are overtaken by a tractor driven by a young woman. Next to the woman, in the passenger seat, sits a big dog. The woman stops at the edge of the road and asks Eva if they want a lift on the trailer. The three climb on to the trailer, which is laden with grain. Someone is already sitting in the grain. He is an elderly, haggard man with dark glasses on. He doesn't speak. The three sit down in the corn. It is a pleasant feeling. Grains get between the leather of their shoes and the skin of their feet. They reach their hands into the grain and let the corn slip between their fingers. They drive towards the sinking sun. The sky is dramatic. The driver of the tractor talks to Eva without looking around. The dog lets its tongue hang out of its mouth and pants. Leonhard takes Magda's hand. Eva drops a few grains into the back of Magda's dress.

After a while the young driver turns into a path, stops in front of a barn on an estate and climbs over the big wheel to the ground. The dog jumps from the seat and runs through the open door of the farmhouse, knocking over a little child. The child starts crying. It's the child of the driver, who immediately picks it up and comforts it. The haggard man with the sunglasses climbs down from the trailer and disappears, without having said a word. Eva thanks the driver.

You'll be coming to the firemen's party, she calls after them. Us village women have already started roasting and baking.

The three walk a short way along the path, then turn into a vineyard and wander between the vines into the valley. The gentle outlines of the hills stand out sharply against the horizon. Now and again the lines are interrupted by the looming vertical black post of a cypress. Lower down in the dusk they see a house with smoke rising from its chimney. They move towards the house. When they reach it it is already in darkness. Lots of people are standing and sitting on the big meadow in front of the house. The party has already been under way for a long time. They are people from the town who have been invited to a friend's birthday.

The wine-growers pour wine for them and sell them the food produced at their farms: meat, sausage, bread, butter.

Magda and Eva know many of the guests at the party, Leonhard doesn't know anybody. They separate and mingle among the people. Eva goes into the house to greet the old farmers. The farmer is small and dainty, his wife big and heavy. While the farmer talks to Eva he watches his four sons, who are serving the guests food and drinks. Eva talks to the farmer while keeping her eye on Magda.

Magda has walked into the open shed. The vehicles have been taken out of the shed and a dance floor has been made for the guests. Three young people from the village stand at one side of the shed playing on a Hammond organ, a little drum-kit and a guitar. They have red music-stands in front of them. Magda sits down on the wooden bench running along the walls of the shed. Glowing torches fixed to the wooden wall light the shed. Beside her sits a woman of about fifty with long black hair and a brightly coloured dress. The woman puts her head in the lap of the man next to her and starts crying loudly. The man is small and ugly and bald.

You have to take life as it comes, the woman says to Magda, crying. It's the only way. You have to take it as it comes.

When she tries to lift her head the bald man pushes it back down into his lap.

A tall brown-haired man pulls Magda on to the floor of the shed and starts spinning her around to the music. She sees the grin in his face and smells his sweat. The man holds her tightly around the waist, looks stiffly ahead and spins her more and more quickly.

Let go of me, says Magda. I can't stand that. I'm getting dizzy.

The man doesn't react and goes on spinning her. Magda breaks away and crashes into a young man with a red parka.

Whoops, says the young man. What's this falling into my arms. Come on, let's go for a walk in the moonlight. It's too noisy here, and everyone's getting drunk.

The young man touches her elbow and pushes her in front of him. They walk through the orchard behind the house and on to the meadow that stretches to the edge of the forest. The nearly full moon shines white above the black line of the tree-tops. Eva stands beside the house and watches after the couple. Leonhard sits at one of the long wooden tables and turns his head towards the disappearing pair.

Eva walks over to Leonhard and sits down beside him. Opposite them, between two beautiful young blonde women who are looking up at him, sits a man of about fifty with a few teeth missing.

My tortoises are the most important thing for me, he says to the blonde women. You have to free yourself from the passions of men. Tortoises are ancient animals. They are very calming. Apart from my tortoises I don't love anyone.

The blonde women nod slowly and lay their heads against his shoulders.

Magda has gone away, Eva says to Leonhard and starts crying.

Yes, says Leonhard and looks into her face. There's nothing you can do. She doesn't stay anywhere.

A shiver runs through Eva.

Are you cold, asks Leonhard, pulls his left arm out of the sleeve of his black suit jacket and lays part of the jacket around Eva.

Magda and the young man have entered the forest. They can hardly see their hands in front of their faces. The young man walks along a narrow path in front of Magda. They walk downhill. He trips over a root and falls. Magda bends down to him and reaches out her hand to him. He pulls himself up by her hand and doesn't let it go. There is a clearing in the dense forest. They are standing in a meadow.

Here is the little pool, says the young man. I know it.

They walk across the swampy meadow. Their shoes sink a little into the wet soil. Magda's left shoe is stuck in the bog. She utters a little cry and balances on one leg. Then she reaches for the shoe with her left foot, finds it and slips carefully back in.

She stands by the pond in the middle of the meadow. Plants with pale flowers float on the dark water. Magda pulls on the young man's parka.

The red dragon, she says. You're the red dragon.

And you, asks the young man. Who are you.

Me, says Magda and laughs quietly. I'm the dragon-slayer.

When Magda and the young man come back the party is almost over. Most of the guests have gone. Empty wine bottles are lined up on one of the long wooden tables. A drunk man counts the bottles. He keeps starting over. Eva comes out of the farmhouse. She's drunk too. She stands beside the counting man and looks at him. With a motion of her hand she knocks over the row of bottles. The drunk man walks to the next wooden table and lies down on it. He folds his hands over his belly and goes to sleep.

Leonhard leans against the outside wall of the shed in conversation with one of the beautiful young blonde women. The woman takes his wrist between thumb and index finger, lifts it up and looks at his watch.

Look, says Eva to Magda, and points at the standing couple. Look. I'd like to go. Let's go.

Yes, let's go, says Magda. The red dragon's coming with us. This is the red dragon.

They walk over to Leonhard and the beautiful young blonde woman.

Let's go, they say. This is the red dragon. He's coming along. He's got nowhere to sleep. He can spend the night on our balcony.

She's got nowhere to sleep either, says Leonhard and points to the beautiful young blonde woman. Can she come too.

No, says Eva and laughs. We haven't enough beds.

No, says Magda and giggles. We haven't enough room.

I'm sorry, says Leonhard to the beautiful young blonde woman. You heard. There isn't room in the house.

The beautiful young blonde woman turns away immediately and walks into the farmhouse.

The four people walk back in the darkness. The moon can no longer be seen. It is behind a long, narrow cloud and is giving it a silver rim. Eva carries her shoes in her hand and walks in the grass beside the path. Sometimes she turns as if dancing. She sings: *Ich hab' die Nacht geträumet / Wohl einen schweren Traum. / Es wuchs in meinem Garten / Ein Rosmarienbaum.* She lies down in the grass and looks up at the cloud with the silver rim. Leonhard walks over to her.

You must stand up, he says. The grass is cold. You could get ill.

The grass isn't cold, says Eva. The grass is soft. The grass is black as night. The grass is a beautiful grave. She sings: *Ein Kirchhof war der Garten, Ein Blumenbeet das Grab.*

Leonhard bends down to her and takes her hands. He draws her up to him.

Come on, let's keep going, he says. Come on.

In front of them walk Magda and the red dragon. The red dragon is singing a different song.

It is a long way. In the darkness they have taken a wrong turning. They have to make a detour. By the time they reach the old house a narrow dark grey strip is visible over the horizon.

Eva walks into the room and falls on to the wide bed. Leonhard goes into the guest-room and closes the window and the door. Magda leads the red dragon on to the balcony. She fetches bed linen and spreads it over a mat in the corner. She turns off the lights and lies down next to Eva on the wide bed. Eva puts an arm around her belly and a knee on her thigh. Magda pushes the arm and the leg away and lies on her back with her eyes open and her hands locked behind her head. Eva tosses and turns uneasily. After a while Magda gets to her feet in the darkness, leaves the room, feels her way through the porch and opens the door of the guest-room. She walks to the bed where Leonhard is sleeping, and sits down on the edge. Leonhard sits up and reaches for her head. Magda resists. Leonhard tries to draw her to him. Magda continues to sit upright.

Stop it, she says quietly. Stop it. It's time for you to go into the big room.

She stands up, goes out of the guest-room and across the landing on to the balcony. The red dragon is lying under the blanket. He isn't asleep. The cat is sleeping next to him.

Come here, he says, throwing the blanket back. I've been waiting for you.

The sun has risen behind the house. It is shining on the table that Eva and Leonhard have laid with plates, bowls and cutlery. Eva is sitting on Leonhard's lap getting dark honey out of a jar with a knife. The knife has a sharp blade. She slowly licks the honey from the knife. Leonhard has put his right ear to Eva's back and blinks in the sun. Magda comes out of the little kitchen with a white porcelain jug full of coffee.

The red dragon has taken his seat beneath the stag's head and is spreading butter on a piece of bread. Magda puts the jug in the middle of the table. The red dragon hands her the bread. The bread and the hands hover over the coffee. The cat jumps on the table.

jonas

The windscreen-wiper moves back and forth. The car drives through the city. You can see the outlines of the driver's head. The rain running over the windscreen dissolves the visible world that the driver is driving into. It's night. Red, green, yellow, white lights move, merge, blur into big patches. The driver pushes a button on his car radio. He moves his lips.

The notes played on the piano rise and fall, rise and fall in clear sequence. In the cinema Jonas slowly moves his head back and forth. He raises his hands and straightens the head-phones of the Walkman, padded with black foam rubber. The car on the screen stops. The driver gets out, locks the car and walks quickly, his shoulders hunched and his hands in the pockets of his brown leather jacket, towards a green neon sign. Cinema Royal. People are crammed together under the porch of the cinema. The man stretches his head searchingly upwards. He walks up to a young blonde woman with long hair. Her hair is smooth and turned outwards at the ends. The woman is wearing a tailored red suit with a short skirt and a white blouse. Her face is that of a girl. The man stops in front of her and smiles. He moves his lips. He closes his mouth. Now the woman moves her lips.

The piece of music ends in a series of notes that get higher and higher. After a pause filled with white noise a new piece begins with three firmly played low piano notes.

Jonas closes his eyes and concentrates on the music for a while. He only opens his eyes when someone pushes past his knees. He sees names appearing in legible capitals at the top end of the canvas, moving slowly downwards and disappearing again at the bottom. The lights go on in the cinema. Each of the three other people who have seen the film with him leaves the room through a different exit.

Jonas walks outside. He is surprised by the brightness of the afternoon. The sky is high and pale blue. A cold wind is blowing. Jonas turns up the collar of his black leather jacket and buttons it up. The Walkman is fastened to the belt of his black jeans. Between the red inside lining of his leather jacket and his grey wool pullover the thin wire stretches diagonally across his torso. A young man whom he knows slightly is waiting in front of the cinema. He says something to him and slaps him on the shoulder. Jonas doesn't understand what he says. He gives him a friendly greeting and walks on without taking the Walkman off. He has the pictures of the film in his head. They are superimposed on what he sees in front of him: a broad street with four rows of cars moving slowly along it. On the other side of the road he walks between the many pedestrians, allowing himself to be pushed and shoved. Someone tugs at his sleeve. It is a small woman with a brown face in a brightly coloured dress. She has a red and gold headscarf wrapped around her head, with a long dark plait hanging from it. On her back she carries a small child. Jonas stops and looks down at the woman. She looks at him imploringly and holds out her palms shaped into a receptacle. Jonas reaches into the inside pocket of his jacket and puts a bank-note into the woman's hollow hands. The woman takes his left hand. She points to the

lines in his hand and says something to him. Jonas thinks
about turning the Walkman down a little. He doesn't do it.
He hears Bach's piano music. The little woman smiles up
to him and takes a crumpled paper handkerchief out of the
folds of her long broad skirt. She shows him a small piece of
glass wrapped in the paper, puts it back in and presses the
paper handkerchief in his hand. Then she makes the sign of
the cross over him and disappears into the crowd. Jonas puts
the present in his trouser pocket and is pushed further along.
He looks into the faces coming towards him. The two faces of
the couple from the film are among them. They appear and
vanish. The people crowd around the light of the pedestrian
crossing. Jonas turns the music up. He doesn't know where
to go. He lets himself be pushed, goes down the steps to an
underground station and gets into a train that has just pulled
in. Opposite him sits a woman in a gold trouser-suit. The
woman is reading a newspaper. THE CIA WAS INVOLVED it
says in big black letters on the front page. The train comes
to a halt underground between two stops. It stays there for
a long time. The people stare ahead. Jonas sees that they
aren't speaking. The woman in the gold trouser-suit reads.
She doesn't turn the page. She lets the newspaper fall into
her lap. She sighs and falls forward on to his knees, then
she slides further and lies beside him on the floor. The train
sets off again. Jonas tries to pull the woman on to the bench.
A man helps him. They lay the woman on the bench. They
put the man's jacket under her head. The woman lies on
her back. Her legs hang over the bench on the side facing
the aisle. Her shoes gently touch the floor with their tips.
They are high-heeled black shoes. Jonas doesn't take the
Walkman off when the man speaks to him.

She'll be better in a minute, he says and gets off.

He walks through the tiled corridors. He sees a man grabbing a woman by the shoulders and shaking her. He stands on the up escalator. He looks at the posters on the walls along the escalator. A beautiful woman in a white cape sits on a white horse. By a brown leather armchair and an open fire, on a shiny brown table, stand a gleaming green bottle and a shimmering crystal glass. A man with a wavy curled wig sits in a judge's gown at the wheel of a Japanese car. A little girl in pink pyjamas bends down to a black cat. A man and a woman kiss by a spring. Two little pigs stand on their hind legs against a low wooden fence and smile.

Jonas steps into the open and walks on. It's quieter here. Some distance away he sees a sign with the inscription AMUSEMENT ARCADE. He goes up to it, opens the door and walks into a big windowless room. The bright lights of the pinball machines shine towards him. Apart from him there is no one in the room. One pinball machine stands next to another. Jonas chooses a machine and puts in a coin. Before he starts to play he turns up the Walkman. He leans his lower body against the smooth front of the machine. Sometimes he picks the machine up a little to guide the ball better into the direction he wants. He wins a free game. He doesn't use the free game. It's occurred to him where he wants to go. He leaves the amusement arcade and turns right. He looks at the windows of the little shops. He sees dusty tins of tuna fish and jam jars. He sees a sign with the inscription MADE TO MEASURE, with four individual shoes and two tubes of shoe-polish next to it. He sees old-fashioned knitted clothes in brown and beige stripes on life-sized dolls with carefully painted faces. He takes an aerosol out of the pocket of his leather jacket. He presses on the aerosol button and holds the tin as he walks so that a long black strip appears on the wall. Under the tracks of the suburban line he stops and sprays the words JOHANN SEBASTIAN BACH on the wall. He covers the whole wall under the tracks with the three words. Despite the loud piano music he hears the quiet sound of the train passing above him.

About fifty metres after the subway he reaches a tall barred gate. PSYCHIATRIC CLINIC it says in an arch above the gate. Jonas pushes it open and walks past a little attendant's cabin. The man in the cabin looks up briefly. Jonas is in a large park surrounded by a wall, with beautiful old houses standing in a square arrangement. Some of the houses have terraces at ground level or glazed verandas. Gravel paths lead from one pavilion to the next. Patches of green with tall old trees stretch between the houses.

Jonas turns down the Walkman. He looks up to the sky. The sun has gone down. The bare branches of the trees stand out blackly against the gleaming red in the west and the television aerials on the pavilions with the flat roofs. Men in light blue pyjamas and striped housecoats, with stubble and grey faces, walk past him. Jonas sits down on one of the cast iron benches. On the bench beside him sit two of these men. One of them rolls up the sleeves of his housecoat and the sleeves of his pyjamas and shows the other one something on his arm. The other touches his arm and opens his toothless mouth in a kind of laugh.

Jonas waits. When the first flock of crows flies over the walls of the institute he takes the headphones of the Walkman off his head so that they lie around his neck. The flock settles on one of the bare trees. The many hundreds of crows on the tree look like leaves. Further flocks pass, spread out, re-form, contract. Jonas spreads his arms along the back of the bench and lays his head far back. The cries of the crows reach his ears from all sides. Gradually more and more birds settle on the trees and on the aerials. The flocks darken the red evening sky. Cries and wing-beats fill the air.

Jonas smiles. He isn't seeing the drama for the first time. Thousands of hooded crows gather here. They sleep on the trees and aerials. The gravel paths, walls and steps are full of their pale dried dung. Jonas sees them getting bigger and bigger. He sees them attacking people with their sharp beaks, flying into their faces. He sees them grabbing people by the back of the neck with their claws, rising into the air with them and flying back to the Russian steppes. He closes his eyes and listens to the music of the hooded crows.

It is dark. Jonas is waiting at a tram stop. He sees the tram coming from a long way off. The tram is brightly lit. Jonas gets on and sits on one of the benches made of narrow wooden slats. It is warm inside the tram. The heaters are switched on under the seats, the warmth rises through the gaps between the slats. Apart from him and the driver there are only two people in the tram. They are two nuns in long dark blue habits. On their heads they wear skilfully folded white cloths. Jonas sees that one of the two nuns must belong to a race from the Far East. She is young and fat and has a round, brown, sulky face. The second nun is about fifty, tall and gaunt. Her eyes are bright and radiant, her mouth narrow, striving upwards at the corners. Her cheeks, forehead and temples are covered with wrinkles. She leans towards the younger nun, puts her hand on her thigh, says something and laughs. Jonas would like to hear their laughter. He has put the Walkman back on and doesn't take it off. He looks out of the window. It has rained briefly, the streets are black and gleaming. As in the film that Jonas has seen, the lights are reflected in the moisture. The face of the blonde young woman from the film appears framed in the window. The red, yellow and green lights of the cars, the neon signs, traffic lights and streetlights move through the face. The face of the blonde young woman from the film reminds him of the face of the girl. Jonas turns up his Walkman.

He and the nuns get out at the same stop. He reaches out his hand to the gaunt nun and helps her over the step into the open. He walks along the street a little way, then enters a pub with a gold boot hanging above the entrance. He is met by noise and fug. He walks to the only free table, a big wooden table without a cloth beside a jukebox. Before he sits down he casts his eyes over the little cards inside the jukebox, some written with a blue ball-point pen, some on an old typewriter. The upper half of most of the typed words is black, the lower half red. The O is almost invisible. The background of the jukebox has a blue glow like fine glass. Jonas puts two coins into the machine and presses the button beside the words AS TEARS GO BY and ROLLING STONES. He can't hear whether the song is played. He sits at the table. A waiter with a fat belly covered by a white apron, a massive head and a heavy double chin props his hands on the table and looks questioningly at Jonas. Jonas orders spaghetti and a beer. The music in the Walkman comes to an end. Jonas takes the Walkman from his belt and turns the cassette over. Then he fastens the player back on his belt. The men sitting at the next table turn towards him and laugh. Jonas eats and drinks quickly. He has taken off his leather jacket. The wire of the Walkman hangs over his pullover. It isn't in the way when he eats. The men at the next table are drinking beer from big glasses. They move their lips and distort their faces. They keep looking over at Jonas. One of the men stands up and comes over. He stops beside Jonas and says something to him. Jonas turns the Walkman down. From a long way away he hears the man's words.

Take that thing off your head, you arrogant bastard, says the man. We don't wear things like that here.

Jonas turns up the Walkman. The man goes on talking, and Jonas can't hear what he says. Jonas guides the last bit of his meal to his mouth with his fork. The man knocks the fork out of his hand. The landlord, who is pouring beer into a glass behind the bar, looks over to them. Jonas reaches for his beer-glass. The man knocks the beer-glass out of his hand. The waiter with the double chin stops mid-movement. The man tries to pull the headphones from Jonas's head. Jonas holds on tight to the wire. The man grabs Jonas by the hair and presses his head down until his forehead and the bridge of his nose hit the almost empty plate. He pulls his head back up. Red sauce runs over Jonas's forehead. He puts up no resistance when his head is pressed back down on to the porcelain. He holds on tight to the wire. He doesn't defend himself. The guests, the waiter and the landlord watch what is happening. They don't intervene. Only when the man lets go of Jonas and walks back to his table does the landlord come over to him and speak to him. He leads him to the door. The man goes.

With a paper napkin Jonas wipes the sauce from his forehead. He gestures to the waiter that he would like to pay. He sees the waiter's gestures of apology. He hears Bach's music. He pays the bill, puts on the leather jacket and leaves the pub. He puts his right hand under his open leather jacket and continues to hold tight to the wire.

Jonas walks through the streets. Light drizzle moistens his skin and his hair. He has turned the Walkman to its highest volume. He sees himself reflected faintly in a shop window. He sees a tall, slim young man with delicate features and pale skin. He chooses a particular direction. He walks through an avenue of chestnut trees. In passing he strikes his hand hard and briefly against a trunk. He walks in the middle of the street. His steps echo on the asphalt. An elegant black car comes towards him at high speed. He jumps aside and feels the car gently graze his hip with its outside mirror. He turns into another street. He takes the aerosol out of his jacket pocket and paints a long black stripe across the walls of the houses.

He stops in front of a tall entrance. He presses one of the bells beside the illuminated name plates. Without hearing whether a voice comes out of the intercom he speaks into the loudspeaker.

It's me, Jonas, he says.

He pauses.

It's me, Jonas. It's me, Jonas. Jonas, he repeats in the rhythm of the music.

He presses himself against the door. After a few seconds the door yields and he is able to open it. Jonas walks past two black rubbish bins and the post-boxes that shine golden in the semi-darkness. The name of the photographer on one of the boxes crosses his field of vision. He walks up the worn stone steps to the first floor and sees the familiar drawing on the wall, the head of a black man with lots of little plaits. He stops at a dark brown door and presses the bell. When the photographer opens he turns down the Walkman. He keeps the headphones on his head.

He walks across the reddish-brown stone floor of the big, high entrance hall. The entrance hall has no windows. The broad white french door to the photographer's living-room is half open. The photographer smiles back over her shoulder and walks through the door. Jonas stops briefly in the entrance hall. A bright pink plastic aeroplane dangles from the lamp in the ceiling. He has bought it at a stall at a funfair, blown it up and given it to the photographer. She has hung it up in the entrance hall. Stacked up in the corner of the entrance hall are a number of old chairs, ripped leather armchairs and some whose seats have collapsed. Against one of the dirty white walls leans a folded stand for drying clothes, against another a tall metal step-ladder. On a wooden chair lies a pile of old newspapers. Empty mineral-water bottles stand on the floor. A big oval mirror is fixed to one wall, beside it hangs a poster about two metres long and one and a half metres wide on which, floating between purple clouds, two men in suits are shown with their mouths open. From the open mouth of each falls the miniature depiction of the other. Beside the high white french door stand a large black umbrella and a small grey umbrella, both open. The loop of the grey umbrella is brilliant red.

Jonas stands in front of the mirror. He hears the photographer calling his name through the opened door.

I'm coming, he answers.

Again he looks at himself in the mirror. He brings his face very close to the glass. His eyes are light green. His lashes are black. He raises his left hand and follows the dark rings under his eyes with his index finger. The skin beneath his eyes is thin. He runs his hand over his cheeks. His face is almost hairless. He lays his hands at his sides and stands bolt upright by the mirror.

That's me. It's me, Jonas, he says quietly.

It's you, Jonas, says the photographer, who has come to stand next to him, and smiles. She too lays her hands at her sides. They look at each other in the mirror. The photographer is small and about ten years older than he is. She wears a white overall. In the mirror they look as though they are the same age. Jonas puts his arm around her shoulders. He follows her into the big, light, almost empty living-room. They sit down at a little table.

I'm tired, says the photographer. Half an hour ago I came back from a fashion show where I'd been taking pictures. Before that I had an appointment with that writer. I made portraits of him in his house. It was gruelling. I found his face very disagreeable. It's hard to take pictures of someone whose face you don't like.

I saw two nuns, says Jonas.

Why don't you take the Walkman off, says the photographer.

No, says Jonas. I can hear you. I understand you.

Two nuns, says the photographer.

I'd like to sleep here tonight, says Jonas. Can I stay.

I'm tired, says the photographer. I've been working very hard. You can stay if you like.

They walk into the darkroom. The photographer's bed is in the darkroom. The darkroom is the only quiet room in the flat. The photographer switches on the red lamp. It casts scant light on the room. The photographer strips off her white overall and lies down on the bed. Jonas takes off his clothes and slips in beside her. He feels for her body. She doesn't pull away. They move slowly. Their naked limbs glow in the red light of the lamp as in the flicker of a consuming fire. Jonas doesn't take off the Walkman. He turns it up. He can't hear the photographer's voice any more. He has put the little black box on the inner edge of the bed. Sometimes it shifts a little. The wire nestles between their two bodies. At one violent movement of the photographer, the wire wraps around her neck. Jonas smiles and playfully pulls it a bit tighter. The photographer sits up. Jonas looks up to her. Bach's music thunders in his ears.

The girl. Women.

They are both frozen in mid-movement. Then Jonas loosens his grip and takes the wire gently from the woman's neck. The photographer puts her head on his chest.

Let's go to sleep, says Jonas.

woman
with three
aeroplanes

Dante and Gabriel are sitting on little chairs at a light blue painted metal table and drinking black coffee and raki. The arms of the chairs touch the hot outside wall of a harbour café. On the floor is a travelling-bag, from whose handles dangle two pairs of tall lace-up suede shoes.

Dante lifts her hand to shield her eyes from the sun.

Look, she says, pointing with her other hand to a ship that's about to set off. The loading platform slowly rises, and at the same time a young woman runs, arms raised, out of the dark hold and up the platform.

I wanna get out. Let me get off this ship. I gotta get off, she calls in English.

The platform lowers again, and the woman runs from the ship with her rucksack. She stops on the pier and turns around. The ship pulls the loading platform in again and slowly sets off. The people on the ship look back over the railing at the island. Some wave.

Stupid bastards, the woman mumbles, as she walks past Dante and Gabriel, takes off her rucksack and sits down at the next table.

Do you fancy her, asks Dante, looking at Gabriel from the side.

Gabriel turns his head, looks at the woman and says nothing.

Do you fancy her, repeats Dante.

No, says Gabriel.

Don't lie. You fancy her.

Not specially. Stop it.

They fall silent and look at the sea. The sea is smooth and calm. The ship moves away, a second appears on the horizon. It is a grey warship.

Yes, Greek coffee. And an egg. Hard-boiled. And some bread, the woman at the next table orders. The waiter chases a few flies with a cloth and says something so quietly that it can't be understood.

Dante stands up. Gabriel takes her hand, opens his knees and pulls her into the space thus produced. He puts his hands on her hips and looks up to her. She stands over him with the light behind her, he can't see her face.

Stupid child, he says, and kisses her quickly on the belly.

When she tries to twist away from him he presses his thighs together and tightens his muscles. At the same time he strengthens his grip around her hips. She fights silently until he lets her go. Then she bends down to him and kisses him lightly on the mouth.

I love you, she says, takes a camera out of the travelling-bag, puts it to her eyes and takes a few steps backwards.

You'll fall into the water, calls Gabriel. She stops and looks at him through the viewfinder. He is sitting leaned back in the chair, in a dark blue shirt whose sleeves reach to the elbows and whose top white buttons are open. His bare golden-brown legs are loosely parted, his feet stretching forward in his sandals. His smooth dark hair is brushed behind his ears and falls almost to his shoulders.

Get on with it, he calls.

How handsome he is. How strange he is. He can barely see me. He's so short-sighted.

In a minute, she says, and swings the camera slightly to the right until the woman appears in the viewfinder. Then she presses the shutter release.

She runs back and kisses him.

You're very photogenic, she says. I love you.

When the ship's siren sounds they empty their glasses and walk on to the ship, which has been in the harbour for some hours. They find a seat on the promenade deck. Two blond young men lie down beside them on a white painted wooden bench, settle their heads on their rucksacks and immediately fall asleep. One of the two is wearing a pair of long white trousers with big black spots, the other a pair with black and white stripes.

Gabriel takes a pack of playing cards out of the travelling-bag.

Let's play, he suggests.

They play for a long time, observed by the passengers around them.

We're playing. We're married. I'm married to this man. Have been for a week. We're putting happiness on display. Are we happy.

One of the blond men wakes up.

We're so tired, he says. We were dancing on the beach all night. We're Danes. Please wake us when we get to Santorini.

He lowers his head back on to the rucksack and shuts his eyes.

Opposite them sit a red-haired woman in her mid-thirties and a pale, black-haired young man.

When I was a child I once got up in the night and put all the flower pots in the apartment around my bed, the man says. In the morning I didn't know anything about it.

You and the full moon, the woman says with a smile.

The man takes her hands, buries his face in them and kisses them violently.

There is a commotion among the people standing at the railing. Dante and Gabriel run across. Before them the great, half-sunken crater of Santorini is opening up. On the left of the water-filled crater rises a dark red cliff wall. The white town lies on it like a layer of snow. At the entrance to the crater dolphins are jumping out of the water. Gabriel points at them.

Take a good look, he says. That's how you laugh. Exactly like that. Like a dolphin.

They return to their seats and eat some tomatoes, cheese and some bread. They drink wine from a half-full bottle in an outer pouch of the travelling-bag. Then they wake the two Danes and go to the exit. They each hold one handle of the travelling-bag. The shoes dangle on either side of the bag.

At the harbour a man walks up to them.

You need a room, he asks.

They agree and drive up the curving road to the town on the load area of his blue van. On the way they pass a group of elderly American women on donkeys. One American woman with bright green sunglasses pointed at the sides has difficulty staying on the back of her animal. She nervously glances back over her shoulder to her friend.

Oh, Carol, I'm falling, she screeches.

The man stops in front of a house right on the cliff that falls hundreds of metres to the sea. The windows of the room that they've been offered have a clear view of the dark water of the crater, a few little black islands and the cliff wall opposite.

Dante and Gabriel stand on the balcony of their room and gaze into the abyss.

In 1956 they had the big earthquake here, says Gabriel, dropping his cigarette butt from the balcony and watching it fall. He goes back into the room and lies down in his clothes on the stiffly stretched white sheet on the wide bed. Dante sits on the balcony for a while. Then she walks to the bed where Gabriel is sleeping. He is lying on his side in a charming curve, his hands against his cheek, his knees slightly drawn up.

She likes looking at him best when he's asleep. After meeting him she waited to see what he would look like asleep. She knew the further course of their relationship would depend on it.

How handsome he is. How strange he is.

Gabriel turns over on his back and starts laughing in his sleep. He opens his eyes.

I was dreaming about a woman who wore a yellow wooden aeroplane as a hat, he says. It looked very funny.

That's why you were laughing, says Dante. Was the woman in the dream beautiful.

Gabriel looks at her and says nothing.

Come here, he says, and spreads his arms.

Dante kneels beside him on the bed. Gabriel puts his

hands under her T-shirt. She closes her eyes and yields to his caress. After a while she takes his hands off her breast.

Did you love her more than me, she asks.

Gabriel leans his back against the wall.

Don't start that, he says.

Did you love her more.

I'm not going to answer that.

Tell me. Tell me, she whispers, curving her fingers and digging her nails playfully into his thigh.

It's hot in the night. Dante can barely sleep. So as not to be bitten by mosquitoes she has pulled the blanket over her head. When she notices that the light is on she pulls the blanket away. Gabriel is standing on the bed with a rolled-up newspaper in his hand, trying to kill mosquitoes. He curses loudly.

I'm complaining to the landlady, he shouts.

Calm down, says Dante.

The next day they hire a motorbike and drive up the coast in search of a quiet place on the beach. They stop above a little white bay. Dante gets off, puts the camera on a stone block at the side of the road and presses the automatic shutter-release. Then she runs back to the motorbike, sits down behind Gabriel, wraps her arms around him from behind and puts her head on his back.

I'm deep-freezing us. I'm deep-freezing our happiness.

They climb down to the sea, carefully clearing a path through low thorn bushes. Halfway down Dante pauses in the shade of a carob tree. The bay no longer looks quite so white. They climb on until they have reached the beach, and lay a blanket on the coarse grey gravel. The tide has brought in sea-grass, which is drying in the sun and smells rotten. Black patches of tar line the edge of the water. In a spot shielded from the wind by blocks of stone there are the remains of a fire and a meal. In the middle of the beach is a crushed red cola can. There is no one to be seen.

They spread out their blanket and walk into the sea. The soles of their feet feel soft plants, smooth stones, the spines of sea urchins. Dante puts her diving goggles on and swims a little way along the coast. After about a hundred metres the beach becomes rocky, the sea deeper. Dante loses the ground beneath her feet. She dives and glides past the rocks. She runs her fingers over the greenish-black, plant-covered surface of the rocks. The plants sway slowly back and forth. Dante feels their feathery delicacy and softness. She presses herself against the rocks, feels her way along them and finds her way into little black bays and grottoes. Fishes swish past her diving goggles. She dives deeper, the water grows blacker and colder. Suddenly she finds herself under an overhanging rock. She is startled and tries to swim to the surface of the water, but bumps her head on the rock before she reaches it. Her breath is running out. She swims around in blind panic. Finally she reaches the surface, shoots out of the water and opens her mouth wide to suck in air. She grabs a protruding rock and holds on tight with cold white fingers. She looks into the sun and closes her eyes. Behind closed lids she watches a red surface run through with fine transparent bubbles like protozoa.

Images from Gabriel's past emerge, from the time before

she knew him. He is walking with a girl through a park in a city. The girl has long dark hair and is carrying a basket of food. She stops, looks up to him, smiles, and pulls him gently into the undergrowth.

Dante sees the slim, long-haired, eighteen-year-old Gabriel beside the driver of a car. The man has thin blond hair and is wearing a dove-grey suit. He looks briefly at Gabriel's profile and puts his hand between his legs. Then she sees him stopping and pushing Gabriel out of the car. In the dark Gabriel creeps to the edge of the road. Yellow headlights come closer, light up his calves and disappear. Immediately afterwards Gabriel finds himself in a cemetery. Between two graves he unrolls his sleeping-bag, slips in and cries himself to sleep.

Dante feels someone grabbing her feet and pulling her under. She cries out. Before she slides into the water Gabriel lets go of her, pulls himself out of the water and lies down beside her.

There you are, he says.

He bends over her face and shakes his wet, glittering hair. She lashes out and he laughs and holds her arms tight. Then he stops laughing and kisses the hollow under her neck. She leans her head back and stretches her toes.

You're so warm, he says, and releases her arms. She lies calmly while he slips the straps of her swimming costume over her shoulders.

They swim back to the sandy beach together. A few yards from their blanket sit two naked girls. Their skin is very white, their hair is very fair. They are talking in a language that Dante doesn't understand. They aren't protecting themselves against the sun. Dante lies down on her stomach, puts on her sunglasses and looks at the girls for a long time.

Beautiful girls. *Déjeuner sur l'herbe*. Careful. The men in the black suits are closer than you think. Careful. No one will protect you. Don't let them near your skin. Their pillaging glances. And the sun, too. At night you will toss and turn in your beds with the heat.

That skin, says Gabriel. They could be Dutch. As if they came from a boarding school.

Was her skin like that too, asks Dante. So tender.

Gabriel sighs, stands up and walks along the beach, with his feet in the warm water, until she loses sight of him. Dante lays her face on the blanket.

She sees Gabriel in a white shirt sitting down with the long-haired dark girl in a field scattered with shrubs. The wind blows through the bushes. Gabriel reaches into the basket of food, opens two red cola cans and hands one to the girl. Then he lays his head in her lap. The girl sits upright and doesn't move.

Dante stands up and walks along the sand, her back bending deep down. She is looking for unusual stones. The two naked girls are talking to each other and pay her no attention. She finds a fairly large stone with a hole through it. There's an animal that bores holes in stones. She returns to the blanket with a handful of stones.

Gabriel has come back and turns and twists the stones in his hand. He takes a pen out of Dante's handbag and starts painting the stones. Here and there he applies a short stroke to stress their shape. A shoe, a shell, a parcel. Dante looks at the altered stones and walks with them to a ten-foot cliff that lines the bay. She stops there and slowly places one stone after another into the little niches in the cliff. Gabriel follows her and considers the work with his hands on his hips.

Let's leave them here, he says. It's our museum. The others will come and look at it. Modern stones.

I'm taking the shoe, says Dante.

Late in the afternoon they walk to a chapel on the summit of a hill. A monk is sweeping the clay floor with a broom. On the altar stand olive-oil bottles filled with lamp oil.

Dante lies down on the narrow bench that runs around the outside of the chapel and draws up her knees. Gabriel walks over to her with the camera and bends over her. When he releases the shutter Dante covers her eyes with her hand.

Stop it, she says. You know I don't like that.

Gabriel sits at Dante's feet.

Why did you marry me, he asks.

To torment you, Dante says with a smile. So that you will leave me again. So that you never forget me.

Snake, he says.

They walk down the hill through vineyards with low vines winding along the ground, and over the white steps of the town. They sit at a table in the square in front of a café with a big plane tree in the middle. The café is called Platanos. The waitress is English. When she serves the coffee Gabriel smiles at her. He takes a serviette and starts to draw on it.

What are you drawing, asks Dante.

The waitress's head.

She's cold, says Dante.

No, says Gabriel.

Stop drawing.

No, says Gabriel and goes on drawing on the paper handkerchief.

The two Danes sit down at a nearby table and wave to them.

I'm going now, says Dante and gets to her feet.

Dante wakes up at dawn. Through the open balcony door she hears a cock crowing. Next to her Gabriel sleeps, his head turned away from her. She gets up and goes to the balcony. The view of the crater is obscured by a fine, light grey veil of mist.

Happiness. How sad. The dark-haired girl. She gives Gabriel a photograph, then she goes. Gabriel goes into a telephone box and calls the girl. He lets it ring twenty times. No one answers. Gabriel walks through the city park in Brussels. He sits down on a bench and takes off his trainers.

Dante walks back into the room and lies back down beside Gabriel. He turns in his sleep and pulls her to him.

What was her name, she whispers.

Gabriel wakes up.

What is it, he asks.

What was her name.

Gabriel lets go of her, sits on the bed with his back bent and opens his eyes wide.

Let me sleep.

Her first name, says Dante.

Gabriel clenches his hands into a fist in front of his face. Then he stretches out his right arm and bangs his white knuckles against the wall. When he pulls them back his knuckles are bloody.

Dante takes the bus to the beach on her own. After looking for quite a long time she finds the same spot as the previous day. The two naked girls aren't there. Dante takes off her clothes and lies down on the blanket. She puts on her Walkman. *In a play / Where the actors die*. The sun shines hotly on her belly. The nearby bushes are fragrant. She gives a start when someone puts his hand over her eyes from behind. She hits the hand away and sits up. It is one of the two Danes. He's wearing red trunks. She takes off the Walkman.

Where's your husband, he asks. What are you looking like that for.

He stayed in the room. He can't stand the heat, says Dante.

I like the heat, says the Dane, playing with the camera lying beside the blanket.

Me too, says Dante.

An aeroplane flies overhead. The Dane looks at it through the viewfinder and presses the shutter.

What are you doing. Stop that, says Dante.

The Dane laughs.

I've taken a picture of you with the aeroplane over your head, he says. It'll be an interesting picture.

Put the camera down, says Dante.

The Dane complies and looks at her. They say nothing. When a second aeroplane appears behind Dante's head, he quickly picks up the camera and presses the shutter again.

The same woman, but a different aeroplane, he says.

Dante pulls her knees to her chest and folds her arms.

You don't do something like that, she says.

The Dane doesn't put down the camera.

Why do you hide your body, he asks. You're very beautiful. You can afford to sit upright.

A third aeroplane rises into the sky behind Dante, and again the Dane takes a picture.

It's a series, he says. Woman with three aeroplanes. You must put the pictures up on the wall underneath one another. You really must.

He gets to his feet. Dante props herself up on her hands on the blanket, and looks up at him, her back straight. In a flash he reaches for her breasts and touches them lightly. Then he runs into the sea and swims away.

Dante gets to her feet and watches the Dane disappear. Then she walks to the water and looks at the hermit crabs. She picks up one of the creatures, which immediately darts back into its house. She sits down in the shallow water, legs outstretched, and lets the waves rock her gently back and forth. She looks at the part of her body that is under water. It looks white and foreshortened.

The dark-haired girl is invincible. She's poured into the past as if in transparent amber.

Dante walks back to the blanket and puts the Walkman on again. She lies down on her back. *In a plane / Going to Helsinki*. When something cold touches her belly she gives a little shriek. She opens her eyes and sees that the Dane has come back and put a cold wet stone on her.

Stay where you are, he says with a smile. I have more little stones in my hand. It's an interesting feeling, isn't it.

Dante keeps calm while the Dane goes on putting little stones on her belly. She feels her abdominal wall sinking beneath the weight.

I'm making a pattern, says the Dane. A cross. A cross on your belly. A cross on your solar plexus. Interesting. Keep still.

The Dane concentrates on his work, making a precise selection, deciding on particular stones. The stones slowly dry on Dante's skin. She enjoys the feeling, and realises that she's becoming dazed. With a jerk she sits up, so that the stones fall off her.

What are you doing there, yells the Dane. You're destroying my artwork.

I'm going now, she says, and slips into her light summer dress.

Gabriel is sitting in front of the house with the landlady, drinking liqueur from a thick, bilious green glass.

Where were you, he asks.

On the beach, says Dante. I was all on my own.

The landlady motions Dante to sit down, and puts down a glass for her. No conversation is possible, as she only speaks Greek. So they say nothing, and smile at each other. The landlady has the tragic look that some Greek women have.

In the evening Dante and Gabriel walk through the town. Gabriel has put his arm around her, and is behaving tenderly. They walk into a shop where Gabriel tries on various woollen pullovers. Dante watches as he moves at the mirror, and as the little salesgirl touches him lightly here and there.

But I can't bear happiness.

He decides for a thick pullover with a blue and white pattern. The salesgirl wraps it in a light blue, rustling plastic bag that Gabriel swings back and forth in the road.

I didn't think I'd find a pullover like that, he says. It's perfect.

In the Platanos café they eat lamb on little skewers and chopped cucumbers with yoghurt and garlic, and drink white wine. Gabriel's face is slightly red, he touches Dante's knee under the table.

Let's go home, he says.

They take the path along the cliff. Gabriel takes her hand and pulls her with him.

Come, he says quietly. I'm looking forward to you.

Dante resists.

Don't walk so fast, she says.

The sun has set. In the west a purple shimmer lies over the sky.

Dante stops. Gabriel walks on a few steps and then turns around to face her.

Tell me the truth, she says. You loved her more. What was her name. Tell me the truth.

Gabriel stands motionlessly. Then he swings his right hand far back and throws the light blue plastic bag in a high arc over the cliff. In the air the pullover falls out of the bag. Dante sees it hit a rocky outcrop far below and go on tumbling until its fall is over. It doesn't reach the water and gets stuck in the brush. When she turns her gaze from the pullover, Gabriel has gone. She sees him running far ahead, until he disappears around a corner.

the
other side
of grief

There is a ring at the door. Paula presses the button that opens the front door and walks into the stairwell. She looks over the cast iron banisters. At first she can't see anything, but she hears men's voices, curt orders, a scraping, a dull knocking. The stairs run spirally down. Paula walks towards the sounds, the shuffling, groaning. She sees the piano-carriers from above. The two of them are carrying the pianino with the help of straps. One, whose bald head gleams up at her, walks ahead, a second behind him. They totter on the stairs, the pianino leans to the side. When they arrive at the beginning of the landing they put the piano on a wheeled board and push it to the bottom of the flight of stairs leading to the next storey. Paula runs down, greets the men, who answer with a tight voice, and walks beside them. On the next landing they put the piano back on the board. The bald man is stocky and at least sixty. The second is younger, blond and weedy, and leans against the wall. He wipes his brow. Paula looks at the older man.

Why do sixty-year-olds have to carry pianos, she thinks.

Man's flesh must be tormented, says the younger piano-carrier as if in response, and giggles. Paula looks into his face and sees the destruction.

The two men go on struggling up the stairs. Paula opens wide the door of the apartment.

Where to, the older one gasps.

She shows them the way to the place that she has chosen for the piano. Then she goes into the kitchen, opens two bottles of beer and offers them to the men, who, standing, put them to their lips and drink them dry in long slugs while their eyes slide over the objects in the room.

She signs the delivery slip and gives them a tip. On their way out the younger man turns around.

Smart place you have here, he says and giggles again.

Paula closes the door, walks to the piano, lifts the lid and strikes a key. A special tone, the blind piano tuner had said, looking past her.

She runs her hand over the wood, the carvings, the places where the veneer has flaked off, runs her finger along a dark circular area on the top. She knows the piano very well. The last time she played it was when she was an adolescent. At seventeen she had given up playing because her piano teacher had seemed more repellent to her from one day to the next.

The telephone rings. It's her mother.

Have they brought the pianino, she asks.

Yes, says Paula.

I told them to treat it very carefully. You can't get pianinos like that any more. It's the frame. The frame is the special thing. A cast iron frame.

It's all fine, says Paula.

I've been lonely since you've been away, says her mother. When are you coming. I'm so lonely.

I'm lonely too, says Paula.

When are you coming, her mother asks again. When you don't come, I'm sad.

Paula says nothing.

Other people care for their mothers. When will you come. Since you've been away I've been taking the pills again. I can't get to sleep without pills.

On Friday, says Paula. I'm coming on Friday. On the evening train.

Yes, says her mother. Other people care more about their mothers. But you were always like that.

I have to go, says Paula. See you on Friday.

Paula looks around the room. The piano is the only piece of furniture. A dark red telephone stands on the floor, the wire snakes across the parquet. Big boxes are lined up along one side of the room. On one box sits a big brown teddy bear with a red headband. Paula goes into the adjoining room. On the floor is a mattress, beside it stand an alarm clock, a half-full bottle of red wine and a glass. A white tiled stove fills one corner.

Paula pours herself some red wine and walks into the kitchen with the glass. The new fittings give off a strange smell. Stuck to the refrigerator is a green label with the word ECOSYSTEM. The kitchen floor is covered with light grey tiles.

Paula has spent the first night in the new apartment. She has planned to remember her dreams. She has dreamed about a child who burst into flames in front of her and burned alive. She was horrified, but then saw that the child was not suffering any harm, that it emerged from the fire unscathed. She wrapped it in her arms.

Paula puts the glass down, looks through a box, finds some music books and walks back to the piano. She opens the carved music-stand, flicks through a music book for a while and puts it on the stand. Standing, she plays a Bach prelude that has stayed in her memory.

Suddenly the little girl is standing in the room.

You have to sit down when you play, she says.

How did you get in, asks Paula. At the same time the answer occurs to her. One door of the room leads to a long balcony that you can reach from the neighbouring apartment as well. A low railing divides it in two.

I climbed over the railing, says the girl. Look.

She leads Paula on to the balcony by the hand and points to the railing.

It's very easy. Do you live here now.

Yes, says Paula, taking two wooden folding chairs that lean against the balcony railing and putting them up. The girl sits on one chair and lets her legs dangle.

A couple lived here before, she says. The man coughed in the night. The woman planted red flowers on the balcony. She sometimes gave me biscuits. Have you got any.

I can have a look, says Paula, goes into the apartment and comes back with a tin. The girl turns over an empty box and puts it between the two chairs.

Let's put the tin on the box, she says. We can have afternoon tea.

The girl puts the tin on the box, opens it and looks in.

I know these, she says. Can I have one. What's your name.

Yes, says Paula. My name's Paula. And yours.

Friederike, says the girl. My mother's working. She'll be back soon though. Wait.

She climbs over the railing and disappears into the neighbouring apartment. She comes straight back carrying a little tray with two gold-rimmed mocha cups, two little saucers with two little spoons and a milk jug, and puts it on the box.

Have you any tea, she asks.

I don't think so, says Paula. I've just moved in, you know.

Yes, I know, says Friederike. I saw the removal men through the spy-hole. Have you anything else.

Apple juice, says Paula. And milk.

That'll do, says Friederike. You go and get the things.

Paula takes a carton of apple juice and a bottle of milk out of the fridge, goes back on to the balcony and puts both on the box. Friederike pours apple juice into the coffee cups. Then she empties the milk into the jug. She pours a little of it into her apple juice and tastes it.

That tastes good, she says. Now we're having afternoon tea. Do you want milk in your apple juice as well.

No thank you, says Paula. How old are you.

Friederike reaches into the tin.

Five, she says. On Sunday we're going to Dresden. To my uncle's. I can write. Can I play the piano.

Without waiting for an answer she takes the folding chair and puts it by the piano. She carefully pushes the keys down.

You mustn't play so loudly, she whispers. What are they for, she asks and points to the pedals.

If you put your feet on them they make the notes longer, says Paula. Try it.

Friederike slips forward on the chair, puts her feet gently on both pedals and carefully chooses the keys.

That sounds good, she says. The notes are getting

mixed up. Like in a magic forest. That's the way elves play.

She goes on playing with concentration. Paula stands at the window with the coffee cup in her hand and watches the child. The girl has medium length, smooth blonde hair. She is wearing a short flowered skirt. Her legs are long and thin, her knees disproportionately large. She is wearing a T-shirt with the impression of lots of little hands.

I have to go now, says Paula. I have to go to the office.

Pity, says Friederike and stops playing. My mother always has to go to the office as well. Can I come back. We can have afternoon tea again. I can bring the crockery. The china.

Yes, let's do that, says Paula.

Friederike walks on to the balcony, puts her things on the tray, climbs over the railing and disappears.

Paula runs along the platform, pulls open one of the train doors which are already closed, throws in her travelling-bag and climbs on. The train sets off. With the travelling-bag in front of her she pushes her way through the narrow corridors of the train, where lots of passengers are standing. She reaches the dining car and decides to stop here and drink a coffee. She sits down at a table where a man is reading a book, gives her order and looks out of the window. From time to time the reading man laughs quietly. Behind her are three noisy drunks.

I tell you what, she hears one of them say. I tell you what now. The wife has to know who's head of the house. That's the most important thing.

The train has left the city behind and crosses a wide plain. Maize fields stretch to the horizon. Paula takes a drink from her coffee.

Am I going in the wrong direction. Where is the right direction. Does the right direction lead away from my mother. Must my mother get smaller and smaller. Is it enough if she waves to me from the distance.

A wonderful book, says the reading man. Finally a book that makes you laugh. That's so rare. It's about this young man looking for his father, you know.

Ah, says Paula.

The tracks rise slowly. Soon the train is high above the valley. Little granaries lie like matchboxes in the green meadows below them. The train enters a tunnel. Paula sees herself reflected in the window.

My sad face. My eyes.

The train comes out of the tunnel again and crosses a high iron bridge. Below flows a frothing stream.

The joke is, says the reading man, that he has at least five possible fathers. His mother had a merry old life.

I see, says Paula.

A merry old life. I'm forty. My life is not merry. I'm not merry. My mother isn't merry either.

On a peak there is a grey stone castle. The train has reached its highest point, the tracks start to go downhill. The reading man claps his book shut, says a friendly goodbye and goes. Paula pays for her coffee. She flicks through a daily paper that has been left on the table. GUEST CRITICIZED MEAL, it says on the front page. AND THE COOK REACHED FOR HIS GUN. She gets ready to leave the train. It stops with a screech of brakes.

Do I want to get out. Or do I want to go past her.

Paula gets out and makes the short walk to her parents' house. Her mother is standing by the front door. She has dressed prettily and had her hair done. Paula embraces her.

She's getting smaller and smaller. Softer and softer. Her skin's getting thinner and thinner.

You must eat something, says her mother. I've cooked for you. Although standing at the stove is an effort for me. I've hurt my ankle. I twisted it in the garden yesterday.

I'm not hungry, says Paula. I had something to eat in the dining car.

But I've cooked for you, her mother insists. You look terrible. The dining car is far too expensive. You must eat.

She turns towards the stove. Paula sees her from behind, the stubborn posture of her shoulders.

Pity and love and rage. There is no escape from this feeling.

In the afternoon they make an outing to Paula's father's grave. People greet them in the street, ask her how she likes it in the city, whether she doesn't miss the village that she lived in for so long, her parents' house, her mother. She gives the answer they want to hear.

Yes, she says. You get homesick.

She sees her empty white apartment in front of her eyes. The girl holding the gold-rimmed transparent coffee cup with her little finger outstretched. She stretches as she walks and smiles at her mother.

Yes, she says, you get homesick. What a lovely day, she says. This clear sky.

Yes, but the wasps, says her mother. The wasps. And the weather won't hold. It's going to rain.

They walk for a while under pear trees. The smell of fermenting fruit from her childhood days.

This is where she came to get me, on this spot. I was two or three years old, I'd ridden my tricycle too far away from the house. Her rage, that is the other side of grief.

For a while the two women say nothing. Paula lifts her head and once again sees the image of the girl cautiously striking the keys. She smiles again.

I have plenty of room in my new apartment, she says.

You don't need so much room, her mother says. Other daughters live at home.

Joy wells up in Paula.

I can go from one room to another, she says happily. The windows are big. A little girl visited me.

You never know with strange people, says her mother. You could have had children ages ago. Where are my grandchildren. I could have five grandchildren.

She links arms with Paula.

Paula pushes her mother's arm away.

You can walk on your own, she says.

They enter the little cemetery and walk through the rows of graves. Many names are repeated. The graves are kept punctiliously tidy.

Look at this grave, her mother says and points to a grave covered with grass. A scandal. If her husband could see that. He suffered so long. And she thinks she can do whatever she likes.

But it was four years ago, says Paula.

Your father has been dead for seven years, says her mother. You have to honour the dead.

And the living. What about the living. She pushed him away. Go away, she said. Her nagging. Her domineering behaviour. Her scenes. For decades. No progress. And now unbounded grief. The new duty. The eternal visits to the cemetery.

Paula looks at her father's picture and calms down. She stands by the grave for a while, hands folded.

Her mother pulls weeds, rakes the earth, waters the flowers and puts a new candle in the lantern.

Let's go, says Paula.

In the evening her mother sits in front of the television and watches the news. Paula reads the newspaper in the kitchen.

Come here, have a look at this, her mother calls.

What is it.

A fire in a dance hall in Madrid. Come on.

I'm reading.

Terrible. All those charred bodies. They're carrying them out. Come and have a look.

A minute.

All young people, your age.

Paula raises her head from the newspaper and looks into a corner of the kitchen. She often took refuge in that corner when her mother was after her. She pressed herself into the space between the fridge and the settee that used to stand there. That was as far as she could get. She stood and waited for her mother, who came closer with her face contorted.

Her glance into the corner shows her the red and blue
weals on her thin child's skin, evokes the shudders she felt
when she ran her hands gently over the gooseflesh bumps to
console herself. Much later she took her mother to task. Her
mother said: if you love your children then you beat them,
that's what I was taught. For Paula this is only part of the
truth. The child felt how her mother enjoyed the beating.
Afterwards she was exhausted and relaxed. The child was
involved in the orgy as a victim.

Her mother stands in the door in a blue dressing-gown.

Do you want a Martini, she asks.

Yes, says Paula and breaks away from the images.

Her mother takes two glasses, half fills them with ice,
pours in some Martini, cuts two slices from a lemon, makes
an incision in each slice and puts them on the rim of
the glass.

I'm taking the glasses on to the balcony, she says. It's
warm outside.

Paula follows her and sits down in a wicker chair. The
moon is in the sky, the spruce tree in front of the house rises
darkly into the air. Farther below is the lake. Lights shine
on the opposite shore.

Why did you go away, asks her mother. You've lived
here for forty years.

That's why, says Paula. You have to change.

She looks at her mother from the side.

She wanted to form a child according to her will. Has
she succeeded.

An apartment is expensive. You could go on living here
for nothing, says her mother. It could be so nice for us.

Paula laughs.

Not on the agenda, she says.

Her mother's tone changes.

Your defiance. You were always unmanageable. You always hung the washing up wrong. I told you, and you hung up the washing wrong on purpose. You were a stubborn child. But I wouldn't have any of it. If you had children you would know how hard it is to bring up children. But you haven't got any. Other women my age have ten grandchildren.

Paula hears herself talking slowly.

It's because of you that I have no children.

What are you saying, cries her mother.

As if you didn't know that, says Paula. As if you didn't know that.

If your father could hear you, says her mother. He would turn in his grave.

Paula hears herself talking quietly.

He needn't have died.

Her mother has risen to her feet. She reaches out her right hand and strikes Paula twice hard in the face.

I'll show you, she whispers. Children must obey. As long as I live, you will obey.

The next morning Paula sets off. Before she goes, her eye falls on the family photographs that hang framed on the wall of the biggest room. From a school photograph her mother looks out at her as a little girl. She has medium-length, smooth blonde hair. She is wearing a white pinafore with ruching. Her legs are long and thin, her knees disproportionately large. Paula stares at the child's face.

That was the beginning. An innocence.

There's nothing to say. When Paula goes her mother is standing in front of the house. Before Paula turns the corner she looks back, sees her mother's back as she goes back in, the stubborn line. Sympathy. She walks on. There is nothing more to be done.

In the train she tries to sleep. As she dozes images rise up. Her mother and she side by side, indistinguishable twins, dark eyes full of grief, her mother and she by an expanse of black water. In a white crinoline her mother strides solemnly into the water, further and further out, her daughter wrings her hands on the shore. Her mother, beside herself, lashing out at her. The rage and the grief.

Excuse me, have you a light, asks the young woman sitting opposite her.

Paula shakes her head.

It's better not smoking, says the woman. I've been smoking since I was ten. I have a shadow on my lung, the doctor says.

With the unlit cigarette in her mouth she stands up and goes in search of someone who can help her with matches or a lighter.

On the way to her apartment Paula walks past a large musical instrument shop. In the window stands a gleaming black pianino, with a black lacquered piano stool in front of it. She walks through the door and sets her bag down. A young man asks if he can help.

I'd like a piano stool, says Paula.

We don't keep piano stools in stock, madam, says the salesman.

But the stool in the window.

It isn't for sale. It's a display model. I'll show you a catalogue. You can order a stool if you like. One month's delivery notice.

Paula sits down at a round table and flicks through a catalogue. She opts for a simple black wood stool with green upholstery.

In her house she opens the first door of the old cast iron lift, pushes aside the second door, puts the bag on the little folding seat and closes both doors. They fall shut with a ringing noise. Paula pushes down the brass lever that says THIRD FLOOR. On her way up she looks through the bars. A prison. A high security wing. DOWNWARD JOURNEYS FORBIDDEN, it says on an enamel plate on the wall of the lift.

Paula meets no one in the corridor. It's very quiet in the house. When she enters the apartment she has a sense of being an uninvited guest. She unpacks her bag, has a shower, changes, makes some coffee and walks into the big room with the bowl. The folding chair is still standing by the pianino. There is an oval object on it. Paula steps closer. It must be a chocolate Easter egg. She picks it up. KINDER SURPRISE it says on the silver foil paper. She sits down on the folding chair and unwraps the egg. It divides easily into two halves. Inside she finds an orange plastic container. The egg consists of dark chocolate on the outside, with white chocolate on the inside. Paula eats one half. Then she opens the plastic container. Little plastic and paper parts fall out. She puts the pieces side by side on the lid of the piano. Long orange birds' legs. An orange beak. She starts assembling the pieces. A big bird. A black and white plastic body. White paper wings. She puts the bird on the palm of her left hand. A heron. A stork. She looks at the bird and starts to cry silently. Her face grows red, she puts her head on the piano lid, her shoulders rise and fall.

After a while she stands up, selects a music book, opens it and puts it on the volume of Bach Preludes. She tries to play one of Bartok's Children's Songs. The notes echo in the empty apartment.

She hears a sound and looks around. Friederike is opening the balcony door.

I heard you playing, she says and sits down beside her. Oh, you've opened my egg already. Can I have the rest.

She picks up the chocolate. Her eye falls on the stork.

Another stork, she says. I've already got three. I must buy my Surprise eggs somewhere else. The man on the corner always has the same things in them. The stork, the pink panther with the tennis racquet and the sailing-boat. Your face is funny. Have you been crying.

I was very pleased with your present, says Paula. But I have nothing for you.

That's OK, says Friederike. You can think about that another time. Today my mother's here. She said I can visit you. Let's have tea again.

Yes, says Paula, that would be nice.

I'll get the china, says Friederike and goes.

Paula sets up the two folding chairs and puts up the box. Then she fetches the biscuit tin, the apple juice and the milk.

Friederike comes back with the tray, and they sit down and eat and drink.

I'm getting a piano stool, says Paula. Then it will be softer when we sit down and play.

That's good, says Friederike. She smiles. Have you a piece of paper and a pencil. I'll write something for you.

Paula finds a block of paper and a ball-point pen and puts them both in front of Friederike. The child tears off a page, shields it from Paula's gaze with her hand and writes. Then she folds the page over a number of times and hands it to her. Paula slowly unfolds it and reads: *Three from me that brings another.*

What does that mean, she asks.

The child opens her eyes wide, pulls her shoulders up and the corners of her mouth down. She doesn't say anything.

Can I keep it, Paula asks.

Fine by me, says Friederike. I can write other things for you.

The phone rings. It's her mother.

I'm worried about you, she says. You looked so bad yesterday. You should spend longer here. The air here is much better than it is in the city. It's a spa.

I'm fine, says Paula. I'm fine.

Your life. Oh, your life, her mother continues. Maybe you're sick. You should be careful at your age.

Paula looks through the window at the bright child's head bent over the box.

I'm not sick, she says. I have to go. I have a visitor.

A visitor, says her mother. You should be careful. Don't forget to put the chain on at night. I have to take sleeping pills. When are you coming.

I don't know. Not so soon. I have a visitor, says Paula, hangs up and walks back to the balcony.

Friederike hands her a new piece of paper, folded together until it's tiny.

I've written you something else, she says.

the
evil
eye

The boy looks at the black woman sitting opposite him in the sleeping compartment. Her eyes are closed and she seems to be sleeping. Her hair has a metallic sheen and is woven into lots of little plaits. Her short skirt reveals part of her considerable purple thighs. Her knees are pressed together, her mouth is open.

The black woman opens her eyes and looks out of the window. At the outside edge of her eyes the boy sees two vertical boat-shaped scars, each about two by two centimetres. They are purplish black, darker than her skin. Like the notch cut with a knife in a tree that has grown in the meantime, he thinks. They must be scars from cuts.

It is growing darker outside the window. One can make out the outlines of high mountains. The train pulls into a station. The door of the compartment is pushed aside, and a girl with a big red rucksack comes in. She takes off the rucksack and lifts it on to the luggage rack. Then she sits down beside the black woman and starts reading a book.

Excuse me, the boy says in English to the black woman. Can I ask you something.

The black woman smiles and nods.

What are those marks, he says and points to the scarred cuts.

The woman continues to smile as she speaks.

It's against the evil eye, she says.

What's the evil eye, asks the boy.

It brings bad luck, says the woman. If someone looks at you with the evil eye you have bad luck until someone frees you from it.

Who looked at you, asks the boy.

An Arab, says the woman. The evil eye is an Arab art.

And who freed you, he says.

An old man from our town. He did it with a knife. The evil eye goes away very quickly if you do it with a knife. I don't have bad luck any more.

The girl has looked up during the conversation. She is about sixteen years old and has medium-length dark hair, a pale complexion and blue eyes. She runs her right hand, which is delicate and slender, along her temple.

Like our Madonna, she says. Our Madonna looks like you.

The boy looks at the girl.

She must be the same age as me. Her hand. That beautiful hand.

What Madonna, he asks.

We have a Madonna in Poland, says the girl. She helped my mother. She's black too. And she has the marks. But only on her right eye. The marks aren't from an old man. They're from the Tartars. The Tartars injured her.

The black woman looks at her watch, stands up and takes her bag.

Goodbye, she says and leaves the compartment.

The girl sits down in the seat that has been left free by the black woman getting off. Their knees touch. They look at each other.

I'm from Norway, says the boy. My name is Magnus.
What's your name.

My name is Lidia, says the girl. Lidia Potocka. I'm from
Warsaw.

The sleeping-car conductor has prepared the compartment
for the night. Two beds are fixed on each wall. Lidia climbs
a ladder to her bed at the top. From below Magnus sees
her taking off her pullover and her jeans. Underneath she is
wearing a white vest with thin straps and white pants. She
slips under the blanket.

Magnus pulls himself up with his arms and falls belly-
first on the other upper bunk. From his rucksack, which
lies behind the head end of the bed, he takes a Walkman.
He puts on the headset, looks for a cassette and puts it in.
He switches the Walkman on, closes his eyes and moves his
head back and forth. He listens for a while, then he takes the
headset off his head and hands it to Lidia.

Listen to that, he says. Listen to that.

Lidia sits up in bed, takes the Walkman from Magnus's
hand and pulls the headset over her hair. The headset pulls
her hair out of her face like a hairband. She can't switch
it on. Magnus slides to the edge of the bed, reaches over
the space with his hand and presses the button. He briefly
touches her hand, which is holding the Walkman. He sees
that she is wearing a slender ring on each finger of her hand
apart from the thumb. He sees the finely ribbed pattern of
her vest. He sees her white, broad, high forehead.

Lidia listens motionlessly, her upper body curved, her
hands on her ears, which are covered by the headset.

I don't like it, she says finally. No, I don't like it. Let's switch off the light.

Magnus switches off the light. They both lie on their backs in the darkness. They get accustomed to it, and can make out the outlines of the window, the beds, each other. They haven't closed the window or drawn the curtain. It is hot in the compartment. The train is going very fast. Lidia hasn't fastened to the wall the leather strap that is supposed to stop you falling.

Magnus's eyes are wide open. He sees a waving blonde woman.

I have escaped Anna. Anna with her fur coats. Am I too old, Magnus, am I too old. No, you aren't too old, you're still young. Am I still beautiful, Magnus, am I still beautiful. Yes, you are beautiful, Anna, you are very beautiful. Anna is thirty-five. She does what she wants with me. She stood on the platform and became smaller and smaller. Her hands reached into the air. Before she disappeared I closed the window. For a year she has been doing what she wants with me. Her hands. The hands that draw my hands under her fur coats. The hands that spread out on my skin. Little padded hands with white fingers. Fat soft fingers with long hard fingernails. There is no antidote to those fingers. The evil eye. The evil hand. But I've got away from her.

In half-sleep Lidia sees pictures. Her father, her mother, her brother are sitting around the table. Her place is empty. Her mother stands up and goes into the kitchen. She crosses herself in front of the picture of the Black Madonna. She lights a thick white candle.

The train takes a sharp bend. Lidia reaches the furthest edge of the bed and holds on tight. She gasps for air. Magnus sits up and stretches his arms out across the space to her. In the dark he clutches a hand. She calms down. She leaves her right hand in his left. Their hands hover above the space.

Get off the train with me, Magnus whispers. Get off the train with me tomorrow morning.

It is half past seven in the morning. The glass door opens automatically in front of Lidia and Magnus. They are standing in the big square in front of the station. They are holding hands. The early morning traffic is dense. The cars move slowly in a number of lines. Even the orange city buses and trams are stuck in the traffic jam. The air is filled with exhaust and the noise of cars.

Magnus pulls Lidia by the hand through the cars, motorbikes and mopeds across the wide street. The blue and the red rucksacks are bright in the morning sun. He pulls her into a little bar whose door is already open, on the side of the square opposite the station.

The barman is short and stocky. Although he is clean-shaven, his chin and cheeks are blackish in colour. Skilfully and quickly he is washing glasses and drying them with a big white cloth.

Practically children, he thinks. Practically still children.

Two coffees and two of those there, says Magnus and points to puff pastries in the glass case.

The barman smiles and winks at them. He puts their order on the table. Then he begins to flick through a large newspaper.

There, he says, and taps a page with the back of his hand. Catania. The Mafia. Every day.

Magnus and Lidia bend over the newspaper and see a big black and white photograph showing weeping women with dark headscarves.

They're everywhere, says the barman. And you, he asks after a pause and winks at them again. Do you want a room. I have a room. Upstairs. He darts his vertical index finger rapidly into the air a few times. Cheap. I don't want a passport. I don't ask questions.

Magnus looks at Lidia.

I'll take the room, he says. A one-bed room.

Two beds, says the barman. It's two beds. But cheap. Like a room with one bed. He looks at Lidia and winks. Lovely room.

Magnus takes Lidia's dangling hand. She pulls it away, picks up her coffee cup with both hands and drinks with her eyelids cast down.

He's taking the room, she says. The room is for him.

Magnus is sitting at the bottom of a wide flight of steps leading up to a church. Far above he sees an unkempt man lying in front of the closed portal of the church. A little girl with dark curls comes down the steps and stands in front of him. She hands him a little picture.

Prende, she says with a dark expression. Take please.

Magnus looks at the brown, crooked, open legs of the girl. Her feet are in blue plastic sandals. Dirty white socks with red hearts have slipped down to the straps of the sandals. The little picture shows a strict-looking Madonna and a Christ child looking like an ugly adult. He shakes his head and gives her back the little picture.

The girl doesn't want to take it, and the picture falls on the stone steps.

Money, says the girl and reaches out her hand. Money.

Magnus shakes his head. The girl spits next to him and runs away without taking the picture back. She runs past a telephone kiosk in which Lidia is standing. Magnus looks at Lidia. She has left the door of the telephone kiosk open. She is speaking into the receiver. She presses one hand against her hip. She takes the hand off her hip and moves it through the air. She puts the receiver down and comes out of the telephone box. She sits on the step beside Magnus.

I've said that I want to look at the city and then travel on to them in three days. That I've found a youth hostel. My aunt was furious. You can't be alone in the city, she said. You're too young. You're only fifteen. I'm sixteen, I said. Then I heard my uncle saying: Leave her alone. I said: See you soon and that's that. That's that.

With her flat right hand she draws a horizontal line in the air in front of her.

Magnus puts his arm around her shoulder. He feels the warm skin on her upper arm. He lays his head on her other shoulder. She lowers her hand and brushes the hair from his forehead. He presses his face, with closed eyes, against the palm of her hand and kisses it.

What sort of picture is that, she says, and picks up the holy picture. A Madonna. That brings good luck.

They walk through the narrow streets. The light falling between the houses doesn't reach the footpath. Only the upper part of the dilapidated walls of the houses catches the sun. Ropes and iron rods run high between the walls and slice blackly through the blue sky. The front doors to the houses are open. They lead straight into dark inhabited rooms. In the semi-darkness an old man in a vest is emptying a plate with a spoon. A woman stands in an artificially lit room at an ironing board and glides the iron back and forth. Little boys stand in doorways and make obscene gestures. People sit crammed in little rooms, cutting shoe-soles out at machines and sewing on gold straps. The back of a black man arches elegantly over a rubbish bin. In one of the little open garages a big young man in a blue overall is working. He has shoulder joints like spheres. But he still looks like a woman. Beside him lie two dogs only a few weeks old. Shapeless women in sleeveless dresses sit with arms folded on chairs too small for them in front of the houses in the shade. Big black birds with brightly coloured beaks in little cages hanging on the walls utter names and make the women laugh and their bodies shake. Collapsible clothes-horses full of wet washing line the alleys. On the corners blue and green neon tubes light grottoes and glass cases with statues of saints and paintings. Dusty and faded plants stand around them. Gold-framed photographs of dead people also lean against the crucifixes and statues.

Look, says Lidia, and pulls Magnus along. I've never seen anything like it.

In one glass case they see little ceramic figures standing on brown plinths. The figures are naked and visible from the navel up. Below that they are being consumed by red ceramic flames. They are women and men, old people and young people, priests and laymen. The figures stand, lit by little lamps, in a red painted papier mâché hell.

Lidia stands motionless in front of hell.

The sinners, she says. The sinners.

In the glass of the case she sees Magnus and herself reflected among the sinners. They are much bigger than the sinners.

But we pray to the picture of the Black Madonna, she says. My brother broke his leg. Then he could walk again. We bought a little silver leg. The vicar hung it next to the Madonna, between all the silver hearts and arms and ears and legs and feet and eyes and hands.

We don't believe that, says Magnus and pulls her to him. My family doesn't believe that. Norway doesn't believe that.

The sinners, says Lidia. Then she falls silent. Magnus doesn't let go of her hand.

On the pavement of a wide street black hawkers have spread their wares out on blankets. Lidia and Magnus stop and bend down to the wares.

Hairbands, says Magnus. I'll buy you a hairband. It's nice when your forehead isn't covered.

Lidia chooses a thick band covered with black velvet. The black salesman with the long, wide robe with the yellow and green pattern puts it on her with a laugh.

Beautiful girl, he says. Good boy. Love love love. That is good. Soon comes death.

He leans back so that his robe billows behind him and laughs loudly.

They cross the streets and turn into an alley that leads upward. The alley soon turns into steps. In the heat they climb up a lot of steps between the walls. On the walls are the ragged remains of election posters, parts of the faces of politicians, maimed, torn faces. Destra nazionale. Destra nazionale. Destra nazionale. Part of these old posters is covered over with six copies of a dark green poster with white writing. Six serious faces of a woman look up and to the left. Over the faces it says Giorni Felici.

Giorni Felici. Giorni Felici. Giorni Felici. Giorni Felici. Giorni Felici. Giorni Felici, Magnus reads out loud. It means Happy Days, he says and pulls Lidia to him. They lean against a low wall and look over the city dwarfed by tall cranes. Some distance away the sea lies grey. Behind it there rises the gentle silhouette of a massive mountain.

The volcano, says Magnus and points towards the mountain. It isn't dead. It's alive.

He looks at the ground.

Like a volcano, Anna always said, taking possession of his skin with her hands. Will you stay with me. Will you stay another little while with me, she asked. He took her hands off his chest. They were hard to remove, like pieces of metal from a magnet.

Will you stay with me, asks Magnus and takes Lidia's head in his hands.

Lidia covers his hands with hers.

Where did you learn English, she asks with a smile. In school.

Yes, in school. And I went on holiday to California twice. I visited a pen-pal. His name's John Hopper.

I was in England, says Lidia. In Kent. With my brother. My parents have friends there. Polish friends who emigrated. In the morning we always went to a language school.

She pulls Magnus by the hand further up the steps to

the portal of a little church. A hand-written sheet of paper is fastened to the wood with drawing-pins.

Corso di preparazione al Matrimonio, reads Lidia. Ultimo venerdí del mese da settembre a giugno. What does that mean, she asks.

I don't know exactly, something about marriage, says Magnus. About preparation for marriage.

He looks at her.

Will you marry me. I'll marry you.

Lidia laughs.

A park stretches across the hilltop. Lots of people are gathered in one part of the park. Some of them are wearing sports clothes. The starting-pistol is about to be fired for a fitness run. Lidia and Magnus see three nuns in black habits with mid-length skirts standing side by side. Each of the three nuns wears a little turquoise plastic rucksack on her back, and on their fronts they have a white plastic bib marked with a red starting number.

Magnus laughs.

The nuns are joining in, he says. How can they run in those dresses.

The nuns are very strong, says Lidia. Don't underestimate nuns.

It's so hot, says Magnus. Let's go into the park. I'd like to sit in the shade.

On a narrow gravel path they walk past white and red oleander bushes towards the semi-darkness of the shady trees. The path widens into a little round clearing surrounded by tall plane trees, with a fountain at the middle.

From a rust-red stone bowl about four metres across the water overflows and is caught in an octagonal basin about eighteen inches high. Lidia stands on the pedestal of the basin and dips her lower arms in the water of the stone bowl. With cupped hands she draws the water from the bowl and wets her face with it. When Magnus comes closer she dips her hands in the water again and strokes his face with her wet hands. Then she takes his hands and dips them in the water. Coins glitter on the bottom of the bowl. Balancing on the pedestal of the basin, Magnus leans towards her and kisses her briefly on the mouth. At that moment a big black dog jumps into the basin so that the water splashes and leaves dark patches on their clothes. They quickly jump from the pedestal and run hand in hand along the narrow gravel path.

Like a big bowl of holy water, says Lidia. Holy water, as much as you like.

There's no such thing as holy water, says Magnus.

Lidia sees her brother pushing open the church portal. He dips his finger in the font. He passes through a wide strip of light that falls from a high window. The silver hearts and arms and ears and legs and feet and eyes and hands beside the miraculous statue flash in the strip of light.

My brother is older than you, says Lidia. He's nineteen. He has black hair, not blond hair like you. He has curls, not straight hair like you. He's taller than you.

Let's sit under the palm tree, says Magnus and points to the unusually thick trunk of a tall palm in the middle of a wide patch of lawn. They walk through the grass to the palm tree and take off their shoes. Lidia leans against the tree. Magnus walks up to her and props his hands on the tree beside her face. He buries his face in her neck.

My brother said I should be careful, says Lidia and runs her lips over his hair. I shouldn't believe what men say. Men tell lies.

Lidia slowly slides down the trunk of the palm tree until she is sitting down. Magnus lies down on his back and tries to force his head between her belly and her raised thighs. Lidia stretches out her legs and pillows his head on her belly. She puts her hand on his eyes. Then she leans forwards and kisses him lingeringly on the mouth. Her hair falls on his skin. She doesn't let his hands touch her while this is happening.

Don't move, she says.

Magnus sees Anna walking through the snow in her thick brown fur coat and her high boots. She gets smaller and smaller. He stands on the threshold of a little wooden house and watches her go.

He sits up.

Where did you learn that, he asks. You must have learned that.

My brother showed it to me, says Lidia. He said I shouldn't let a man do that.

For a long time Magnus says nothing.

What's your brother's name, he asks.

His name is Andrzej, says Lidia.

Let's go, says Magnus.

Without saying a word they walk out of the park and down the steps on the other side of the hill. From a window on the third floor of a house a little girl lowers something small and light on a noose. Magnus takes it out of the noose. It is a little home-made envelope, sealed with red sealing-wax. He looks up to the little girl. The girl calls furiously down to him. As he walks on, Magnus opens the little letter. Inside it is a piece of paper on which, in made-up child's handwriting, there is a letter with a date, a salutation and a signature. Only the signature is readable. It is the name Chiara in capital letters. A woman has come to join the child at the window, and she scolds him as well.

You shouldn't have done that, says Lidia. You shouldn't have been so curious.

They walk back to the bar in the darkness. They pass an old church with a crumbling façade, which houses an elegant department store. Through the glass doors of the former church portal they see shop-window dummies dressed in leather jackets. The entrance to the bar is brightly lit and open. Noise comes from inside. Football fans, dressed in red and white, are celebrating the victory of their team. They are young people, there is only one older man among them. He is carrying a red and white striped banner with the name of the team and, despite the heat, a red woollen hat with a white bobble. He is drunk and singing.

The barman greets them with a laugh.

The room is ready, he says. Beautiful bed. Beautiful bed. You can go and sleep. He looks at Lidia.

We want to eat something, says Magnus. Do you have anything.

I can do a toasted sandwich, says the barman. Do you want a cheese and ham toasted sandwich.

Yes, please, says Lidia. Make two. And I'd like a beer.

Magnus pulls Lidia close to him. They look around. Beside them at the bar stands a man of about thirty, drawing something in a book. He holds the pen with his fist and draws so violently that he tears little holes in the paper. The tip of his tongue can be seen in the corner of his mouth. He draws with various coloured pens. He keeps casting glances at Magnus. A blonde woman of about fifty with a long frizzy pony-tail puts her arms around a young football fan. She has a cigarette clenched between her bared, bad teeth. When she blows smoke into his face he pushes her away. She lets the burning cigarette fall from her mouth and kicks it outside with a furious movement of her right foot, so that her pony-tail swings back and forth. Her eye falls on the young couple standing embracing at the bar. She laughs out loud, points at them with her finger and says something that they don't understand but which makes the people in the bar burst out laughing.

It doesn't matter, it doesn't matter, says the barman, when Lidia buries her face in Magnus's shoulder. Nice people. All nice people.

He puts the toasted sandwiches on the smooth stone surface of the bar.

There it is. Good toast. Just a bit. Just a bit before you go to sleep.

He giggles.

The drawing man tears the page out of the book and gives it to Magnus. They look at the muddle of orange and green lines on the paper. There are a lot of eyes scattered around in the muddle. When Magnus tries to give it back the man gestures that it is a present.

Don't take it, says Lidia. Those eyes.

Magnus puts the drawing in his trouser pocket.

He'll be pleased if we take it, he says. Why not.

After they have eaten the barman takes the rucksacks that have been behind the bar all day.

I'll show you the room, he says. Come on.

He guides them up a narrow flight of stairs to the first floor, opens a room with a big key, puts on the light-switch beside the door and makes an expansive gesture with his arms.

Goodnight, he says. Goodnight, mes enfants.

He puts the rucksacks on the floor and goes back down the stairs.

They look around the room. The grey concrete walls are bare, a lightbulb hangs from the ceiling on a long black wire. In one wall there is a little window with no curtains. Beneath it is a bedside table. To the right and the left of the bedside table are two beds. At the foot of the bed on the left stands a chair. Three black coathangers hang on a loop fastened to the wall with nails. Beside the door a little white wash-basin protrudes from the wall. A wide crack runs across it. Above the basin, on a porcelain shelf, is a water-glass. Beside it is a little piece of soap. A white towel hangs on a hook in the wall.

Beautiful room, says Lidia and starts laughing. Magnus joins in the laughter and jumps on the bed.

Beautiful room, beautiful bed, he shouts, and falls on his back on the bed. Then he gets a bottle of red wine out of the side pocket of his rucksack. He takes a knife out of his trouser pocket, unfolds a little spiral bottle-opener and pulls the cork out. He stands up, fetches the water-glass and fills it to the brim. He hands it to Lidia, who is rummaging in her rucksack. Lidia drinks half of the glass and gives it back to him. When he has completely emptied it, he pours in more wine and drinks again.

Lidia goes to the light-switch and turns off out the light. Because of the faint greenish glow from the street the room is not in complete darkness. Outlines can be seen.

I've got to wash, says Lidia.

Magnus vaguely sees Lidia getting undressed and putting her clothes on the chair. He hears water flowing into the basin. He sees Lidia holding her face over the basin. He sees her stretch her arms into the air, bend over, stand up again. He finishes the second glass of wine and pours again. He walks to the light-switch and turns the light on. Lidia stands naked in a puddle of water on the floor. She has narrow shoulders and wide hips. Her breasts are small. He turns the light off again, puts his arm around her shoulders and leads her to the bed which is untouched.

I'll marry you, he says.

Lidia lies in bed with her eyes open. She thinks that it must be five or six in the morning. Magnus is pressed against her shoulder and has laid an arm over her torso and a bent leg over her thighs. It makes her feel stifled. She doesn't dare move lest she wake him. She can only see a little part of Magnus's face. His hair hangs over his forehead, his mouth is open. He breathes deeply.

So that's it, thinks Lidia. It's not so important.

She carefully tries to free herself from Magnus's embrace. He moves and tries to pull her to him again.

I can't sleep, she whispers. Let me go to the other bed.

Stay here, murmurs Magnus. Stay here, I'll marry you. He goes back to sleep straight away.

Lidia stands up and sits down on the other bed. Magnus has now wrapped his legs and arms around the white sheet. On the sheet are two red patches, a big one and a small one.

For about a quarter of an hour Lidia sits straight-backed on the bed. Then she gets dressed, takes her ruck-sack, quietly opens the door, doesn't close it and goes down the stairs. The front door is locked, but a woman cleaning the floor in the bar opens it for her. Before she steps out into the street, the woman smiles and pinches her cheek.

On the big station clock she sees that it is just before six. She crosses the street, still almost empty of cars, and walks to the station. The glass door opens automatically and she walks into the station. In the station stands a big white-haired man in a green parka. He throws his arms in the air and shouts something filled with rage up to the glass roof of the station. She has the impression that he is constantly repeating the same sentence. Two young men sitting on their sleeping-bags in a corner are laughing at the man.

He's been robbed, one of the young men explains to her in English. He's had his bag stolen. Do you want a sandwich. We have coffee in the Thermos flask as well.

No thanks, says Lidia. I haven't got time.

She runs her eyes over the board with the departure times of the regional trains and discovers that the next train to the little town where her uncle and her aunt live departs in two hours. She leaves the station hall and strolls diagonally across the station forecourt. She turns into a narrow street because she sees stalls of fresh fish. The salesmen are setting up the market. Pulsating shellfish lie in the water in big bowls. Bubbles rise to the surface. A black eel twists across the table and hangs over the edge. Slender greyish-blue fish gaze at her from enormous round eyes. The fish sellers try to persuade her to buy something. She doesn't react and rounds a corner.

In front of the façade of a church stands a plane tree. From a depression in the trunk of the plane tree grow fig branches with fresh leaves. Lidia walks into the church. On a tall metal scaffolding stands a young woman, painting at a fresco with a fine brush. The colours of the left half of the painting are pale, those on the right are glowing. Lidia stops by a little Lady altar. A young, beautiful Mary with a blue robe and a smiling child on her arm looks back at her. Lidia takes her wallet out of her rucksack, puts a few coins into the slit of the box under the statue, puts the wallet on the altar and lights a thick, short white candle in a red glass container. She prays for herself and for no one else. She smiles at the kind Madonna and leaves the church. She goes on walking aimlessly through the streets and finally walks through a gate in a wall into a big garden. It's a rose-garden. Roses of all colours are blooming over a wide area. A scent wafts towards her. She walks through a tall rose trellis. The roses twine together above her head. On a bench beneath the roses sits a dark-haired woman of about forty who looks like an Indian, in a long, black and white flowery dress and wearing light-brown glasses that give her face a catlike quality. The woman has one arm over the arm of the bench, she holds her chin high and her head inclined, and looks from the hill over the roses and the houses of the city that can be seen beyond the wall.

She feels good in her solitude, thinks Lidia. I would like to be like that woman.

Suddenly she feels a pang of joy. No one has to walk through the trellis with her, no lover, no bridegroom. She wants to walk alone through the marriage trellis.

She doesn't need anyone.

Slowly she walks back to the gate and out of the garden. In a little bar she orders a coffee. On the wall behind the barman's head hangs an old sepia framed photograph showing the bar in 1923. The man in the photograph looks very like the barman. When Lidia is on the point of paying, she notices that she hasn't got her wallet. She tries to explain to the barman, the barman understands and lets her have the coffee for nothing. Lidia thinks that the wallet must be in the church, on the altar. There is no other possibility. She walks back to the church and pushes open the portal. A slim young man walks towards her. Lidia looks the man straight in the face, certain that he has her wallet.

Did you find a wallet on the Lady altar, she asks in English, then in Polish.

The young man looks at her and shakes his head with a smile. The scaffolding that the young woman was standing on is deserted. In one of the pews at the back kneel three nuns in burgundy habits with snow-white wimples. Lidia sits down in a pew.

Magnus runs down the stairs and pulls open the door to the bar.

Where's my girlfriend. Have you seen the girl, he shouts.

The barman, who is drying glasses and talking to a man

with dark blond hair, a pale, bad complexion and a brown leather jacket, turns his head towards him.

I don't know, he says with a smile. I haven't seen her. Maybe she's gone for a walk. It's nice in the morning.

You're responsible too, shouts Magnus. I'm calling the police.

The barman steps out from behind the bar and puts a hand on Magnus's shoulder.

Wait. Wait a while. Perhaps she's gone for a walk. She'll come back. You'll see, she'll come back. Go to the room and wait for her.

Magnus runs outside. He runs through the streets where they walked the previous day. After a while he gets slower. In a dark, narrow alley lined with houses ready for demolition a handsome young man sits amidst the rubbish on a rubbish bin. He doesn't see Magnus. Magnus sees him filling a syringe and pressing the needle into the bend of his outstretched arm, wrapped round with a tourniquet. As he walks on Magnus begins to cry. The dark alley opens into a wider one, and this in turn into a little treeless, deserted square. Magnus sits down on a bench.

Beside the bench, by the wall, are two stone plinths. The figures of two stone women recline on these plinths. Both are leaning on their elbows. One statue is in good condition, the second badly damaged by time and the weather. On this figure, which was clearly once very similar, the head and arms can only be very vaguely discerned. It looks as though a veil has been placed over the woman's body, as if she was sinking, dying, into the stone plinth. Magnus's gaze slips again and again from the statue in good condition to the damaged one. His face distorts in a pain with which he is unfamiliar. He goes on staring at the statues. He stops crying. He starts looking at the two statues in the reverse order. A woman slowly rises out of the stone. She turns from a sketchy figure into a sharply outlined woman with arms and hair.

Magnus stands up and goes on looking. He walks past a church with a plane tree in front of it. In an alley, in front of the crumbling wall of house, he sees a girl from behind. The girl is Lidia.

Magnus, she says. Look.

Magnus walks beside her. Behind a pane of glass is one of the papier mâché hells. Reddish brown, uneven walls with little cave-like depressions rise up. Along the reddish-brown floor run thin wires leading to empty black lamp-sockets. That's all. The burning ceramic figures have been taken away.

Lidia looks at Magnus.

Hell is empty, she says quietly.

as
a
stranger

The unknown man is standing there again. On the other side of the street. He is leaning in a house doorway and holding a bouquet in silk paper in his hand. He is wearing a dark blue velvet cap.

Gerda is opening the gallery. It is eleven o'clock in the morning, a Monday. She raises the blinds. She has arrived on the night train from Vienna three hours before. She has looked around various galleries there and organised an exhibition with a young Viennese painter who makes large-format paintings in finely graded shades of white.

I don't understand how people can use those different colours so carelessly, the painter said. It would unsettle me. White tones are confusing enough. Disturbing, he added, and looked at her, his eyes wide with fear. God yes, she thought, nodded, and cast her eye over his body under the white shirt with the wing collar and the big sleeves, under the white linen trousers. She is forty-six.

She shared the sleeping-compartment in the night train with an Austrian woman who was going to the International Catholics Day. A critical priest was going to be delivering psychoanalytic lectures on the fairy-stories of the Brothers Grimm. She had a lot of respect for this priest, said the Austrian woman, once he had almost been excommunicated.

Gerda slept badly. It was hot in the compartment, and

when she opened the window a crack the airstream blew in, and the sound of the moving train seemed to get louder and louder.

People jostled at the station. They carried big cardboard boxes or sat on them. She took the underground train past abandoned stations. Faintly lit, subterranean swimming pools with no water. Wonderful settings for a spy film. Tiled cemeteries. Get out here, that's what I'd like to do.

The door of the gallery opens, and the unknown man walks in. He stops before a big painting showing the shadowy figure of a woman. The painting is called Grey Bride. The man is middle-sized and gaunt, his face birdlike and delicate. He turns around and puts the bouquet with the paper in front of her on the table with the catalogues.

This is for you.

I told you I didn't appreciate your presence.

But I love you.

Go.

The unknown man comes up to her and takes her by the wrists.

You belong to me, he says. I'll get you.

She breaks away, runs to the door and bumps into a woman who is just coming in. The visitor apologises and begins flicking through the catalogues. The unknown man goes. She sits down on a chair.

What does he want. I know what he wants.

She has taken no measures against him. For about two weeks he has been coming to the gallery almost every day after watching her from the street. Then he always comes in when she's alone. He hardly ever says anything. Once when she asked him what he wanted, he answered: You know very well. Sometimes he tried to touch her.

An acquaintance comes into the gallery.

I need your car, he says. Just for an hour.

The guy was here again, says the gallery-owner.

Call the police.

It's not necessary.

She gives him the keys and the papers, and he goes away again.

The unknown man stands beside the glass of the big window of the gallery on the pavement. By now there are three visitors in the three rooms. The gallery isn't going well. She has invested a lot of money. The art market is a hard thing to predict. The man smiles at her through the glass. A visitor wants to know how much the value of the works in the exhibition will rise over the next five years.

Three times, she says.

At three o'clock Lisa comes and takes over.

I've left Max, says Lisa.

The guy is standing outside the window again, says Gerda.

For good, says Lisa.

Gerda takes her jacket, leaves the gallery and walks past the unknown man.

I'm so in love, he says.

She doesn't answer. He walks along beside her.

I'll get you, he says and stops. I'm going to get you.

She eats in an Indian restaurant. There is just enough

room for four little tables. At the next table sit a bleached blonde woman of about thirty and a dark young man with wavy hair.

He's getting out of hospital on Friday, says the man. He has to go back to Istanbul.

What's it all for, she says.

He reaches for her hand over the table.

No, she says. We don't suit one another.

Gerda stands up and walks home. She takes the path through the park. Children have climbed on a telephone box. She looks around for the unknown man, he's nowhere to be seen.

The danger his feeling puts me in. Sometime I'm going to have to call the police. It's still too early. I'm going to get you.

Her apartment is in a quiet setting. In the bakery next to her house she buys two pieces of cake. There is a bill for the repair of her washing machine in the post-box. No letter. For weeks she's been getting anonymous letters with black and white photographs showing her. Standing by a phone box, crossing a street, flicking through a book in an antique shop.

To see what I look like to others.

In one of the photographs she is sitting in a pub garden, in conversation with an acquaintance. Laughing, with lively hand gestures.

I like myself, as a stranger.

She opens the locks of her apartment door. Tired from the journey she lies down on the sofa in her work-room, after moving the pile of newspapers on it. While she is putting the newspapers on the wooden floor beside the white tiled stove, she reads the headlines: TWO CHILDREN CATCH FIRE AT BARBECUE.

The ringing of the telephone rouses her from her sleep. Her mother is complaining that her sister won't look for regular work. Her mother won't stop talking about her sister.

But what's it got to do with me. What's it got to do with me, thinks Gerda.

Her electricity's been cut off, says her mother. She was just here and wanted to shower. I didn't let her in. And I'm not going to pay her electricity bill. Please speak to her. Can't you use her in your gallery.

She doesn't tell her mother that she is in financial difficulties herself. Her sister isn't reliable enough, she answers, she knows what her sister is like, what she's always been like. She always has these grand plans that never come to anything. She promises her mother that she will speak to her sister.

A man's taking photographs of me, she says. In the street. Without my knowing. He sends them by post.

Your sister is a failure, says her mother. There are a lot of crazy people.

Gerda walks into the kitchen, makes coffee, pours it into a big bowl, sits down with it on the balcony and eats the cake out of the paper. Down in the street brightly dressed women and children walk around begging. They go into the houses as well. There is a ring at the door. A little girl stands there making a pleading gesture with her hand and her eyes. Gerda is annoyed at the disturbance, shakes her head and closes the door. Halfway to the balcony she stops.

My cold heart.

She takes her purse and opens the door of the flat again. The girl is nowhere to be seen. She walks on to the balcony and sees her coming out of the house.

She leans over the railing.

Hey, she calls. Wait.

The girl looks up at her. She throws her a five-mark piece. It falls on the footpath. The girl bends down for it and doesn't say thank you.

I've given a girl like that nothing once before.

She waters the flowers and the herbs and gets changed. And she sees her face in the mirror.

There's something in it that led the unknown man to choose me for his madness. My madness.

She drives to an exhibition opening in the centre. A lot of people have come, the usual public. Black crows. An architect she knows slightly introduces her to a Hungarian and a Colombian writer.

The Hungarian takes his big hat off and says: I live in Budapest. I have two daughters. Sometimes I write for thirteen hours a day. I have no iron. You look as though you have an iron. Do you sometimes iron. Lend me your iron. I have no iron in this city.

The Hungarian looks like a Swede. The Colombian looks like an Arab. He doesn't say much. The architect laughs a lot. In a corner the painter stands playing the trombone.

He has an apartment with a view of the Hudson River, says a woman in a red dress beside her. He only paints on plywood now.

Gerda takes a glass of wine and stops in the niche of a window. The architect walks past her with a man.

It refers to Warhol, of course, the man is saying to the architect. Every single song's about him. It's a wonderful album.

The Hungarian joins her.

We're going to drink champagne today, he says. There's a café a few houses along.

The Hungarian's accent gives her a sharp pain. His voice, a soft knife.

And I don't have an ironing board, he says. Lend me your ironing board.

The Colombian stands with his hands on his back in front of a picture. A woman walks up to him and says:

Didn't you live in Rabat. I know you. I gave birth to my third child in Tangier. I wanted to visit Bowles. The child came too quickly. Bowles is eighty. He goes walking a lot. He looks at spiders. How do you like the paintings.

A man keeps coming into my gallery, says Gerda to the Hungarian writer. He sends me photographs. He's peculiar.

Peculiar, says the Hungarian. You are peculiar. Let's drink champagne. I don't like these paintings. Were you ever in Gyula. The full moon over Gyula is like the full moon nowhere else.

A black-haired girl comes up to him and kisses him lingeringly on the mouth. He has a fish's mouth.

Good to see you again, says the girl. I'm so happy. Call

me. Please call me. But only in three weeks. I'm going to Mali tomorrow morning. We're all so unhappy here. Good to see you again.

Then she goes down the stairs.

The catalogues are sold out. Gerda walks with the Hungarian, the architect and the Colombian to the café near by. The Hungarian orders champagne. He starts reading from his book in Hungarian. After a while she takes the book from him and tries to read out loud as well.

One can understand you, says the Hungarian.

She doesn't want to stop reading. While the men talk she goes on reading out loud, without understanding a word.

At some point they leave the café. The waiter runs after them into the street because the Hungarian has given him too much money. On the pavement they shove the bank-note back and forth between them until the Hungarian finally takes it.

They go on drinking in the Café Phoenix. The Hungarian says to her: I will go home with you.

Go home with me, Gerda repeats.

The architect is asleep beside her. The owner walks up to their table.

Sleeping at the table is forbidden, says the owner.

He isn't bothering anyone. He's sleeping peacefully, she says.

He shouldn't sleep peacefully, says the owner.

It is growing light outside. In the Green Café the Hungarian orders champagne again. They are sitting on a balcony over

the street. A man is dancing in the street with a thin white
scarf around his neck, which reaches to the ground. Gerda
half closes her eyes, the light of the rising sun hurts her.
The Hungarian sits down at the next table and tells three
young Swabians about the plain around Szeged.

The full moon over Szeged is like the full moon
nowhere else.

The three young Swabians are here for the meeting of
Catholics.

Nothing against Swabia, says a Swabian and moves his
head slowly back and forth. I invite you all to Swabia.

The Colombian is silent for a long time, then he stands
up, politely takes his leave and goes. Gerda strokes the head
of the architect sleeping beside her. The Hungarian pays,
and they walk on with the three Swabians. They sit down
on wicker chairs in front of a café, Gerda leans her head
against the warm wall of the house. It's mid-morning.

We in the Catholic movement are cheerful people, says
the second Swabian. We like to sing.

Yes, people in Swabia like to sing, says the third
Swabian.

The three Swabians write their addresses down beneath
one another on three pieces of paper, and give the three
pieces of paper to the Hungarian, the architect and Gerda.

See you in Swabia, they say and go. The architect
disappears as well.

I know where you can get a good goulash, says
the Hungarian. A very hot Hungarian goulash. Come.
Come.

They walk for five minutes to a little bar on a corner.
They are the only people there. The Hungarian orders

two goulashes from a young waiter. Two older waiters sit with their backs to the wall on either side of an occasional table. They yawn at the same time. When the young waiter brings the goulashes he smiles at his reflection in a big mirror on the wall. They eat the goulashes slowly.

Excuse me, says the Hungarian and giggles. But perhaps you will kill yourself. It could be.

Perhaps you will kill yourself, she says.

Excuse me, he says. But you have never loved.

What can I do, she asks.

Love is very close. You can see nothing.

When they have eaten the goulashes they pay and go to the ice-cream parlour on the opposite side of the street. The waitress is gaunt and looks like a famous actress.

We would like two longing cups, says the Hungarian to the waitress.

The waitress smiles.

What do you mean, she asks.

You know, longing cups. A creation. He makes a hand movement. Longing, he says.

I understand, says the waitress.

She brings the longing cups. The longing cups are made of thick light blue glass, with the pastel colours of the balls of ice-cream visible inside them. In one bowl is a long wooden stick with a bright silk paper butterfly, in the other a red plastic rose. They eat the ice-cream.

I will go home with you, says the Hungarian.

It won't be necessary, says Gerda.

I will go home with you anyway, says the Hungarian. He waves to the waitress.

They take the underground to Gerda's apartment. Beside the front door the unknown man is leaning against the wall.

I've been waiting for you for ages, he says.

Yes, she says, opens the door and walks into the house.

Sorry, says the Hungarian, follows her and shuts the door.

death's
heads

The young woman stands under the shower. Smiling, she massages the shampoo into her long blonde hair. She raises her face towards the stream of water and lets the water run over her face with her eyes closed. Her eyelashes are long, her mouth red and full, her nose delicate, her teeth regular. The contours of her shoulders are soft, her skin is slightly tanned and supple.

The young woman walks through the city in a short red dress. Her legs are long, slim and straight. She is wearing black shoes with high heels. She is carrying an expensive-looking handbag. Her glossy blonde hair swings slowly back and forth. Along the street stand tall young men in elegant suits. They are carrying briefcases, and cast admiring looks at her. A man with dark curly hair whistles after her.

The young woman opens a door and walks into a room in which well-groomed men and two well-groomed women are sitting. She smiles radiantly and looks at the clock.

Edith gets up from the sofa, walks to the television and switches it off. Then she sits down again and takes a drink from the glass that stands beside her on a table. She puts it to her mouth and looks at the skin on the upper side of her right hand. The skin is as thin as crushed tissue paper and scattered with little brown blotches. The veins protrude clearly.

Edith puts the glass down and picks up a newspaper from the table. She flicks through the newspaper, showing the new fashion in swimming costumes. Tall, slim, well-proportioned photographic models are standing with long legs in the desert sand, their slim necks stretching towards the sun. Their bodies are firm and immaculate.

Edith shuts the newspaper. She stands up and walks through a door on to a balcony giving a wide view of the city. On the slightly sloping meadow in front of the house the new grass is coming up. Yellow primulas and blue liverworts grow beneath the shrubs along the fence. Under the balcony a girl in a skimpy pink bikini is sitting in a green and white striped deckchair. She has one foot on the front strip of the deckchair, and is painting her toes bright red. Between the bright red toenails of her other foot are little rolls of paper. The girl's thick black hair is casually pinned up with a gleaming red hairgrip, revealing a beautiful neck and the thin straps of the bikini tied into a bow.

Edith turns around, leaves the balcony, takes the glass, drinks it dry and walks out of the room and through the corridor into a little dark room. She drops on to the wide bed that stands in it. She turns to the wall and draws her knees close to her body. She bends her elbows, clenches her fingers into loose fists and touches her forehead with them.

Outside the closed door a dog barks. The doorbell rings. Edith starts from her dozing. She opens the door to the room. A little dog jumps yapping up to her and runs ahead of her down the steps to the door of the flat.

Who is it, asks Edith before she opens the door.

I'm terribly sorry, says a young male voice.

Edith opens the door a crack. The dog slips out. A handsome face with green eyes smiles at her. She has seen the face many times before.

I'm terribly sorry, says the young man who is standing on the top step of the short flight of stairs leading from the door of the house to two tall white apartment doors standing next to each other at right angles. I pressed the wrong bell. I wanted to see Inge. Inge Zernatto.

The dog jumps up to the young man. It wags its tail. The young man tries to stroke it.

No, Edith says sharply. He could bite.

He doesn't look like it, says the young man. What kind of dog is he.

He's a she. A dwarf spaniel.

Pretty colour.

You scared me, says Edith. It's not nice to be woken from your sleep.

I'm really sorry, says the young man, and turns to the other door, which has opened. The girl stands on the threshold in the pink bikini. She is tall, her skin seems to have a golden brown shimmer in the light from the door.

I wouldn't have opened the door, says Edith, but I was waiting for a visitor as well.

Hi, Peter, says the girl and reaches her arms out to the young man. Then she sees Edith standing in the door.

Hello, Frau Schneider, she says in a friendly way. Did he ring your bell first.

A visit from my boyfriend, says Edith.

The young man has stopped paying her any attention. Edith shuts the door and walks slowly back up the stairs. When the dog won't stop barking she gives it a shove with her foot and says: Be quiet.

She walks back into the living-room and takes a file out of the bookshelf. She sits on the sofa and opens the file. The file contains photographs. In one photograph a girl in a glittering sleeveless dress is dancing with a serious-looking young man in a dark suit. The couple moves among other dancers. The girl is young and beautiful and smiles with white teeth. Her hair is cut very short, giving her neck a virginal appearance.

That was me.

She goes on flicking. A young woman is sitting on the stump of a tree. Her long slim legs are crossed, and she is leaning one elbow on her knee and her chin is in her hand. The sun is shining into her face, her eyes are narrowed to little slits. The wind has blown one strand of her long hair into her face. Through the narrow slits the young woman is looking at someone. She is smiling at someone.

That was me. My mother didn't tell me how beautiful I was.

Edith stands up and walks to an oval mirror hanging on the wall beside the bookshelf. She turns on the two white, trumpet-shaped lamps to the left and right of the mirror. The light of these lamps is not soft. She walks up to the mirror and looks at her face for a long time. It is tanned, her skin is dry and covered with lots of big and small patches of pigment. Horizontal wrinkles are buried in her forehead, not deep, but there are many of them. Her neck also bears two wide, washed-out rings of wrinkles. Edith lowers her head. The flesh on her cheekbones is a little loose. She runs her hand over it. It is very soft. The surplus flesh under her chin is also tender and yielding. The pores in her chin are highly visible, as are the little hairs on her upper lip. Edith pulls a thick, short black hair out of the corner of her mouth. She shows her teeth. Above the canines in her upper jaw the gums have receded very far. The lower incisors are short, worn, brown with tartar. Their arrangement is irregular. Some of her incisors are blackish. She opens her mouth wide. Some molars are missing, the others have big fillings. The middle four incisors in her upper jaw are the finest. They are crowns.

The teeth of a death's head. The death's head is all that remains. A clean, hard white death's head.

She turns off the lamps and walks to the open window, below which stands the desk. The big magnolia tree outside is covered with white blossoms. Some of them lie on the grass below. Inge Zernatto is standing in her bikini leaning against the trunk. She puts her hands behind her and holds on to the trunk. She stands on tiptoes. In front of her, two or three metres away, kneels the young man. He is turning the lens of a camera.

Good, he says. That's good. Now go behind the trunk.

Inge steps behind the trunk, wraps both arms around it and looks out from behind the tree with her head on one side. She smiles.

Edith stares at the smiling girl.

Stay like that, calls her friend. Stay that way.

The girl smiles and smiles under the blossoming magnolia tree.

Edith sees Richard opening the garden gate, closing it and coming up the gravel path to the house. He waves to the two young people under the tree. She walks down to the door of the flat, again accompanied by the dog. She opens the door.

Hi, Edith, says Richard, who is standing at the door with a flat parcel wrapped in white tissue paper with gold writing. I've brought rolls. Is that OK.

Hi, Richard. Come in.

The dog jumps up to Richard. It whines.

Stop that, shouts Edith. That's enough.

Leave her alone, says Richard. It doesn't matter to me, you know that. I like it.

Edith pulls the dog into the kitchen by its collar and closes the door.

They walk into the living-room. Edith takes the paper off the rolls and puts the big rectangular cardboard plate on the table beside the sofa. She fetches a second glass and pours wine from the half-full bottle. She sits down on the wicker chair beside the table. Richard lowers himself on to the sofa, picks up the glass and drinks.

How nice it is here, he says. I've been in the studio almost all day. The radio play's nearly finished now. When are you going to do something again.

This documentary about old actresses will take another while, says Edith. It isn't easy digging up all those mummies in their various old people's homes. And then they sit in their wheelchairs talking such nonsense that you can only use a fragment of it.

Richard takes the second roll.

Edith looks at him. He's tall and has curly grey hair and the slight beginnings of a paunch. His eyes are dark brown.

The girl on the ground floor, says Edith. She's very beautiful, isn't she.

She's very young, says Richard. They're all beautiful then.

Actors are the stupidest things alive, says Edith.

Not all of them, says Richard.

Yes all of them, says Edith.

What's up with you, asks Richard and pulls her beside him on to the sofa. He puts his arm around her shoulders and strokes her face with the other. Edith sees her old hands lying in her lap. Between two buttons of Richard's shirt there is a little gap through which she sees the grey hairs on his chest.

She breaks away from Richard and stares ahead of her.

What's up with you, says Richard.

I'm ugly and old, says Edith.

That's not true, says Richard. You're not ugly. And you're not old. Why don't you believe me. I've told you often enough. Not many women look as good as you in their early fifties. I think you're really feminine. Very attractive. You know that. Why are you moving away from me.

I can't. Not any more, she says. And quietly after a pause: And I'm short of time. I still have to prepare the media course for tomorrow.

Richard looks at her. Let me stay here, he says. Let me spend the night with you.

I'm short of time, she says. You should go now.

Richard stands up and looks at the cardboard plate with the rolls he brought with him. Almost all the rolls are still there. He has eaten two of them. Edith hasn't eaten any.

Edith looks up at him.

You know the way, she says. You'll find it on your own.

Richard walks from the room and closes the door behind him.

Edith hears the dog barking from the kitchen. For a while she sits on the sofa, then she stands up and walks on to the balcony. She briefly sees Richard's back. Then he turns the corner. She walks back into the room and stops in front of the desk. She looks at the papers lying on it. Before she sits down at the desk she looks out of the window. Inge Zernatto and her boyfriend are sitting on the little terrace ringed by red geraniums. In front of them on the little table are their empty plates. There is a little salad left in the bowl. Crushed paper towels lie on the white table-cloth. Inge is wearing a thin, flowing blue dress. Edith can hear fragments of words, their laughter. Inge stands up and sits on her boyfriend's lap. Edith looks from above into the cleavage of her dress. Then the cleavage disappears behind her boyfriend's head. Edith sits down at the desk.

Edith sleeps fitfully. She sees a tangle of intertwined young bodies. A tangle of snakes. Richard comes and reaches into the middle of the tangle.

They're not dangerous, he says.

Edith stands up and fetches a glass of water. The dog at the door makes a long groaning noise. She lies back down in bed.

The girl's bed is directly below hers. A glass floor. Looking through a glass floor. She floats above the bed of beauty, an evil ghost, a death's head ghost barely covered with flesh. Inge's dark hair radiates like a star, a black star. The arms at her sides are outstretched, her legs opened. There is nothing between Inge and her apart from the glass floor, apart from her own glass bed. Then a shadow passes between Inge and her. The shadow of her boyfriend. The boyfriend covers Inge. The boyfriend covers Inge completely.

Edith drinks the last drop of coffee. The dog looks up to her. It has shining brown eyes. The dog loves her. The dog doesn't mind about her decay. The dog is stupid. The dog wags its tail. The dog wants to go out of the house with her. As punishment for its stupidity it isn't allowed to.

Edith closes the kitchen door, behind which the dog whines. She leaves the flat. On the gravel path she meets Inge Zernatto. She is pushing a bicycle. She is wearing tight jeans and a loose T-shirt.

Good morning, Frau Schneider, she says in a friendly way. Isn't it lovely today. I've been running already.

Good morning, says Edith. Running. I never run.

My boyfriend doesn't like it either, says Inge. It's too strenuous for him.

My boyfriend likes running, says Edith. My friend can run for miles without getting tired. He's in very good physical condition.

Yes, says Inge. Running is very healthy.

She pushes the bicycle back up the gravel path.

The morning light blinds Edith. On a narrow asphalt road she walks past beautiful old houses with big gardens. Now and again a car comes towards her or overtakes her. It is a quiet, expensive district. The earth in the flower beds has been freshly dug. Little brightly coloured flowers are blossoming everywhere. The light is the light of spring, a flashing brightness. Yellow blossoming forsythia bushes explode everywhere like beacons. The fruit trees stand in the gardens like white torches.

Edith turns into the university campus. She walks into the main building and up a flight of wide stone stairs to the first floor. About twenty students are sitting in the little auditorium. The young eyes, the young faces look at her. Thick manes of hair, smooth bare arms, protruding Adam's apples, delicate shoulder-blades. Beardless cheeks. Roundnesses. Relaxed muscles, tensed muscles.

Edith walks up to the wooden lectern and puts her book of notes in front of her. She begins to speak. Her mind isn't on it, and she notices that she is reading a lot from her notes.

She goes home a different way. A way that doesn't lead through so many gardens. She walks past billboards, up to billboards. Enormous red women's lips far above her head. Ankles beside her, half a metre across. Curving insteps above huge red shoes with high high heels. Silk stockings metres high. Skin skin skin. Green eyes blue eyes. Lance-like lashes far above.

A young woman holding a child by the hand walks past her.

Look at the lady, says the child and turns around towards her. Look at the lady.

Edith walks quickly. She sees the house where she lives. She stands in front of it. She opens the green garden gate. The gate bangs shut behind her. A few steps in front of her Inge's mother is walking up the gravel path to the house. She has a key. She opens the door and walks in to her daughter's. Closing the door, she turns around and sees Edith.

Hello, Frau Schneider, she says. Wonderful weather, isn't it. And glorious flowers around the house.

Yes, says Edith and closes the door to her flat behind her.

The dog jumps down the steps to greet her. She pushes it away and goes into the kitchen to give it some food. While she is chopping up the meat the dog licks her ankles. She pushes it aside with her foot and puts the bowl on the floor.

Eat, she says. Eat, now.

The dog eats quickly. When the bowl is empty it looks up at her. It hasn't got enough.

That's enough, says Edith. Don't be so greedy. It was enough.

She walks into the bathroom to change her clothes. On one wall of the bedroom stands a mirror about two metres high. She opens the windows. She gets undressed and stands naked in front of the mirror. She stands so close to the mirror that her belly almost touches the glass. She grasps her belly with both hands and between her fingers she pushes the roll of fat running across her lower belly together so that it protrudes even more. The blue-veined skin seems tense to bursting-point. Her navel disappears deep into her flesh. She lets go of her belly and dangles her arms at her sides. Her arms are long and disproportionately slim in comparison with her wide hips, on which there are little bumps of fat. She leans her head slightly to the side and looks down at her thighs. The surface of the skin is uneven, forming little shadows. She runs her finger tips over her thighs. Under the skin she thinks she can feel cartilage. In the light of the room her skin looks pale, greenish. Her knees are not well formed. Her calves are slender, but not straight. Her eyes slide back up along her body. Her shoulders are high, gaunt, bony. Her breasts are a little misshapen, a little saggy.

Edith stands there motionlessly.

The skeleton beneath. Beautiful and hard.

The phone rings. Edith slips into a black housecoat and walks to the phone. It's Richard.

How are you, he says. Are you better.

I'm fine, thanks, she says. Thanks, fine. The dog's a bit tiresome sometimes.

Do you want to go to the pictures, he asks. Do you feel like it. A Japanese film.

Not today, she says. I've got to work. Another time.

The film's supposed to be very good.

Not today. OK then.

Bye, Edith.

She puts down the receiver and walks into the living-room. A rose. She saw a rose in a film by Kurosawa. The dark-red velvet rose covered a large part of the screen. Soft, soft. Dark shadows between the individual petals. A column of black ants moves up the stem to the flower. Evenly. Not stopping. Moving up the stem, the thorns. They are so small that the thorns do nothing to them. Climb over the points of the thorns. Press into the centre. The innermost. Destroy the innermost. The innermost beauty. And the gaze of the boy watching the column of ants that begins some distance away from the rose on the ground.

She walks to the window above the desk. Down on the terrace Inge Zernatto is sitting on a kitchen chair. Around her shoulders is a white towel. Her black hair is wet and reaches her waist. Behind her stands her mother, combing it with slow movements. She uses a big comb. When Edith sees her mother's movements she begins to cry.

What hair you have, says her mother. Such beautiful hair. Thank God you didn't inherit mine. Such thick hair.

Inge doesn't move her head and hands her mother a pair of scissors over her shoulder.

You can cut a few centimetres off, she says. The tips have started to go. Cut them off.

But it's a shame, says her mother. Such lovely hair.

Edith walks back into the room and sits on the sofa. The tears run down her motionless face.

In a dream Edith sees a young Japanese woman sitting on a straw carpet in the corner of an empty room. Her right hand is on the remote control of a television. Beside her on the floor is a little bag embroidered with silver. She is wearing a blue kimono. Her lips are bright red, the rims of her eyes and her eyebrows are painted black. Her hair is combed strictly back. There are pearls in her ears. She has a dark expression. Suddenly, with awkward hands, she tears open the kimono above her breasts. Then she pushes up the kimono to her belly, so that only a little strip of fabric, about thirty centimetres across, covers her upper body. Her legs are fat, her feet are in white cotton socks.

Look at it, she says. Look at everything. It's edible.

Edith turns from one side to another. She is hot under the blanket. She throws the blanket aside and sits up. Her eyes gradually accustom themselves to the dark of the room. She looks at the clock beside the bed. It is four o'clock in the morning. Without any particular intention, she stands up and walks from the room. She notices a smell. She can't immediately identify the smell. She looks down the steps to the door of the flat. The wall along the stairs is full of paintings. A pig standing by an abyss looks at the moon. A wolf follows a girl in a red cape. Edith blinks. She takes a deep breath. She sees fine smoke rising up the stairs. She recognises the smell.

There's a fire, she thinks. Where's the fire.

She walks down the stairs. The smoke becomes a little denser. She walks back up again. She walks into all the rooms and can't find anything. In the kitchen the dog raises its head and makes a brief sound. She walks back down the stairs. She notices that smoke is coming through the door of the flat.

There's a fire on the ground floor. There's a fire at the girl's flat.

She runs up the stairs to the phone. She reaches out her hand to take off the receiver and call the fire brigade. Call the girl. She pulls her hand back. She stands motionlessly. She walks back into the bedroom and quickly gets dressed. She takes a jacket out of the wardrobe. She walks into the kitchen and fetches the dog. She walks down the stairs with the dog, and out of the flat. Acrid smoke is pouring through the gaps between the door of the girl's flat and the wall. She leaves the house with the dog. It's dark. On the gravel path she fastens the lead to the dog's collar. She walks through the garden gate. She sets off for the city centre.

The city is deserted. A drunk approaches, taps his hands at her and utters incomprehensible words.

Clear off, says Edith.

You're getting me wrong, darling, you're getting me quite wrong, says the drunk.

A van stands in front of a bakery. The door to the loading bay is open. There are baskets of bread in it. Two men carry a basket to the bakery. The drunk walks unsteadily up to the van and takes a roll out of a basket.

Hey, hands off, calls one of the men.

Only some of the windows of the shops are lit. The beautiful slim shop-window dummies with their long pointed fingers are in the dark. Long, thick black hair falls in the dark down the shoulders of the beautiful shop-window dummies. Their faces can hardly be seen, their red lips are not red. The extravagant gestures of the shop-window dummies. The swing of their hips. Black outlines.

In the east the horizon is turning light grey. The stars are fading. The moon moves through black clouds.

A big orange refuse truck drives through the streets. The truck stops. Men in orange overalls noisily tip the black bins into the truck. An old man with a thick white moustache walks past her with an Alsatian. He nods to her.

She walks past the opera house, across the farmers' market. Some farmers are setting up the wooden tables on which they arrange their fruit and vegetables. The loading areas of their vehicles are open. On a bench in front of the Opera House two young people sit in a motionless embrace.

Edith turns off the wide street and into an avenue. She walks into a meadow with the dog. The dog lifts its leg against a tree-trunk. A man stands not far away from her near a little glazed cabin. It is a weather station. His hands are crossed on his back, and he looks at the curves that the pointed indicator draws on the slowly moving rolls of paper. He turns around and walks past her.

The air pressure is rising, he says to her. The humidity is falling. And the temperature is also rising. Finally.

She sits on the bench and watches it getting light. The dog trots through the park meadows.

When Edith walks through the garden gate the paper boy is coming towards her. He is wearing a yellow rain jacket with red writing, and under his red and yellow cap he has a light grey scarf wrapped around his head.

Terrible business, he says and shakes his head.

Has something happened, asks Edith.

There's been a fire. The ground floor looks bad, the paper boy says and walks on.

Edith sees the black triangles over the windows of the ground floor. She lets the dog off the lead. The dog runs along the fence. Edith walks up the gravel path. The door of the house is open. The carpet that covers the short steps to the door is wet through. There are traces of soot on the walls. The french door to the flat on the ground floor is open. She can see through the flat to the terrace door that is also open. Edith walks through the front door, climbs the steps and walks into the girl's apartment. The paper is burned away from the walls and hangs in scraps. Edith walks into the living-room. A confusion of wetness and blackness. Only charred remains are left of the carpets and wall hangings. Some of the books on the shelves are burnt, the rest are covered with soot. The walls are black, the doors, the door handles. Three white patches gleam at her from the wall. They are the three sockets of an electric plug. Edith walks to the window. The cord that opens and closes the blinds dangles black above the windowsill. The windowpanes have become opaque. The stereo system has melted, its straight lines curve. In one corner of the room the fire has eaten deep into the wall up to the ceiling, and the parquet floor is also burnt away. At some points on the wall there is an old layer of red paint that was hidden under the white walls. The beautiful ceramic oven is half covered with soot. Each of the big tiles is decorated with the relief picture of a knight with a lance. Against the background of the old red layer of paint the knights look as though they were riding into a sea of flames.

Edith walks a few steps towards the bedroom. She holds her breath. She sees a black shadow. It is the bed. She walks through the opening of the door into the room. The bed has burnt down.

At a little round table with a stone table-top sit

Inge Zernatto and her boyfriend. A bottle and two little glasses stand in front of them. In the glasses there is a transparent fluid.

Hello, Frau Schneider. We need this schnapps now, says Inge Zernatto. Do you want a glass too.

Edith approaches silently. She sits down on a chair.

It could have been a lot worse, but luckily no one was at home. Where were you actually, asks Inge Zernatto.

Me. I was taking the dog for a walk. Sometimes when I can't sleep I take the dog for a walk. It must have been about half past three when I went out.

And you didn't notice anything, no smoke, no smell of burning, nothing, asks Inge's boyfriend.

No, says Edith. I didn't notice anything.

It probably wasn't burning yet, says Inge, facing her boyfriend. Then she turns to Edith.

An electrical fire, the fire brigade said. Dangerous wiring. We could both have suffocated, you and me both. Or burnt. You and me both.

Then she turns to her friend.

All three, she says.

She turns back to Edith.

Such good luck that he phoned me, she says. In fact he wanted to spend the night at my place, you know. But then he called me, quite late, about eleven, and asked if I didn't want to cycle over to his, he was too tired to come. Then I got the bike out of the cellar and set off.

She laughs and runs her hand over his hair.

You bring me luck, I know.

And who called the fire brigade, Edith asks quietly.

Our neighbour. She works in a nightclub and came

home at about half past four. I know her, I sometimes visit her with my mother. She tried to phone me in the flat. When there was no answer she called the fire brigade. And my mother. My mother then called Peter, because she thought I might be at his place. We came here on our bikes, and the fire brigade was already putting it out. Nothing at all has happened in your flat, the fire brigade said.

All this damage, says Edith. Such damage.

We'll see, says Inge's boyfriend. Maybe the insurance company will pay. It's quite possible that the insurance company will pay for the damage. Then you'll have a new flat, he laughs and looks at Inge. You were always saying you were going to give the place a complete overhaul soon.

How lucky, says Inge. Do you want another schnapps.

No thanks, says Edith and stands up. I'm going to lie down for a bit. See you later.

The police will be here later in the morning, Peter calls after her.

Edith walks in front of the house, calls to the dog and walks with it into the flat. She shuts the dog in the kitchen. She closes the kitchen door. She hears the dog scratching at the kitchen door. She walks into the living-room. She runs her hand through her hair. Her eye falls on the oval mirror. She sees her hand in the mirror. The skin is as thin as crushed tissue paper and scattered with little brown blotches. The veins protrude clearly.